prizefighter
en mi casa

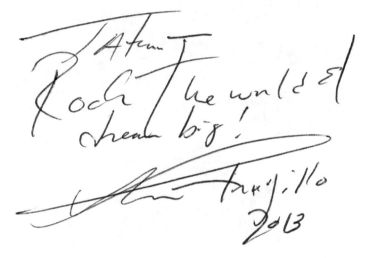

To Aaron
Rock The world &
dream big!

Trujillo
2013

prizefighter en mi casa

e. E. Charlton-Trujillo

DELACORTE PRESS

Published by
Delacorte Press
an imprint of
Random House Children's Books
a division of Random House, Inc.
New York

Text copyright © 2006 by e. E. Charlton-Trujillo

Jacket illustration copyright © 2006 by Matt Mahurin

Visit us on the Web! www.randomhouse.com/kids
Educators and librarians, for a variety of teaching tools, visit us at
www.randomhouse.com/teachers

Library of Congress Cataloging-in-Publication Data
Charlton-Trujillo, e. E.
Prizefighter en Mi Casa / e. E. Charlton-Trujillo.
p. cm.
Summary: Following a car accident that left her with epilepsy,
twelve-year-old Chula—with a little help from a visiting
fearsome Mexican boxer—tries to deal with the repercussions
her new condition has on her family, neighborhood, and school.
ISBN: 0-385-73325-9 (trade) — 0-385-90344-8 (glb)
ISBN-13: 978-0-385-73325-0 (trade) — ISBN-13: 978-0-385-90344-8 (glb)
1. Self-acceptance—Fiction. 2. Epilepsy—Fiction. 3. Traffic
accidents—Fiction. 4. Boxing—Fiction. 5. Family problems—
Fiction. 6. Schools—Fiction. 7. Mexican Americans—Fiction.
PZ7.C381855 Pri 2006
[Fic]—dc22   2005013214

The text of this book is set in 11.5-point Baskerville.

Book design by Angela Carlino

Printed in the United States of America

August 2006

10 9 8 7 6 5 4 3 2 1

BVG

For Pi

prologue

He wasn't what I expected at all. Not really. Not really at all I guess. With his low brow and dark skin. Not the way Abuela talked him up. "Dark as Death," she'd say. "Darker."

In the darkness, he could've been mistaken for something darker I guess but not Death 'cause this thing, the Cacooey the neighbors called him, he had skin.

Skin that fit him like caramel that had been out in the sun too long and dried up in places and chiseled in some harder shape. He was a thick man the size of a bear with broken dusty knuckles and one eye covered with a chewed-up patch.

I knew the stories of the Cacooey since I was little and like a lot of the kids in the Circle walked faster to get home when it was dark. 'Cause that's when the Cacooey would find you. In the dark.

But I never imagined that night when he came to our door that he would actually be a kind of Mexican I'd never thought of before.

1

a gutted pumpkin glowed from across the street. The streetlight closest to the house got shot out almost one whole year ago so I could barely see nothing. Nothing but that glowing orange head without a body.

I sat on the porch swing hoping to stay outta Mama's way. She was in one of those moods again where she cursed the saints she'd be praying to later. Being Mexican and Catholic requires a lotta prayers. Even if they never seem to be answered you're still supposed to make 'em. But I'd quit that after all the glass.

The latch on the gate banged shut only I couldn't see nothing but a shape, a moving shadow with footsteps. Footsteps that made the porch stairs cry and moan. It walked right past me sitting on the swing and knocked on the screen door. I sat there all quiet but the swing squeaked. The Shape turned toward me. I didn't know what it was but it was big. Really, really, really all kinds of big.

The porch light flicked on and the Shape winced and fell back a step. Like when you go out into the sun after being somewhere really dark.

Mama opened the screen door saying "Hector" over her shoulder to my father.

Mama and I kinda stared. I couldn't believe that was the man my father believed was our family's gold.

The wheels of Pape's chair grinded against our wood floor. "Come in, come in," Pape said from inside the doorway.

Mama held the door open and took the Dark One's suitcase as he slipped inside.

"Chula," Mama said. "Get off the swing and get in here."

I started shaking my head.

"Andale," she said. "I'm not telling you again."

I pushed off the swing and went to the door.

"What did you say to him?" she asked me.

"I didn't say him nothing."

"Listen. Like it or not, that is all we have. God help us," Mama said. "So don't do anything to upset him. ¿Bueno?"

I stood there not saying nothing.

"What? I don't have all night," said Mama. "Get in here."

I ducked under her arm and followed her into the kitchen.

"Get the iced tea," said Mama.

"Hello, Abuela," I said to my grandmother.

Abuela leaned back in a chair at the kitchen table. Smiling, with her hands crossed in her lap. Her eyes half-open, half-closed like cats when they go to sleeping. Only she wasn't sleeping. Not really.

"The tray, Chula," said Mama. "Come on."

Mama poured a bag of Tostitos into our sort of fancy lime-colored plastic bowl. She stepped around me and grabbed the homemade picante sauce out of the fridge.

"It's staying with Tío Tony, right?" I asked her.

"He. His name is El Jefe and that is what you and your brother are to call him," said Mama.

"Or he might do worse than kill us," my dumb older brother Richie said, strutting into the kitchen all tough-like. "He might box our ears off so we can't hear nothing."

"Shut up," I said.

Richie grinned, chomping into a chip.

"No sir," Mama said, pulling the bowl away. "This is for El Jefe."

"Pues, you see the size of that guy?" Richie asked Mama. "He's like the Mexican Hulk."

Richie stuck his hand back in the bowl and she slapped it.

"¿Qué pasó?" asked Richie.

"No jokes. No nothing," said Mama. "This man has come a long way to help this family." Then she looked at me. "And he's staying here."

I looked at her like she'd just lost her mind.

"Cool," Richie said.

Mama walked over to Abuela and squeezed her hands. Abuela didn't do nothing. Not even blink. If her chest wasn't moving up and down, I would've thought she done died. Done died right there in South Texas dreaming of Mexico.

Mama turned on the radio. We only had one in the house and it played only for Abuela. Sometimes she'd get to looking too distant from us and closer to God, and Pape didn't like seeing his mama like that. The music seemed to return part of her to us, even if it was only for a while. But one thing I learned about *a while* in my family, it was never very long but it was longer than never and you always have to aim for that. Never means nada and nada means nothing and we want more than that, Mama always says. You must always want more than your history.

Mama weighted me down with the tray of cups and iced tea. Richie scooped up the bowl and salsa and we followed behind her.

Pape was smiling and happier than I'd seen him in like forever when we came into the living room. Mama stacked the magazines and free TV guide from the neighbor's Sunday newspaper under the coffee table so she'd have a place to put tea and chips.

"I'm sorry," said Mama to the Dark One. "We weren't expecting you until tomorrow morning."

He nodded but didn't take his eyes off the floor. Really his eye 'cause he only had one. The other was under a dusty patch with clawlike scars that went up all high on his head and spread outta the bottom like crooked fingers. I wondered if they hurt as much as the one on the side of my head.

Mama took the tray and chips from me and Richie and I stood there still looking at the creature out of the corner of our eyes. No way could it be true that Pape useta stick up for El Jefe when he was little. How could that Cyclops ever be that small?

Mama leaned in and said to me and Richie, "Sit down on the couch *now.*"

Richie walked around the coffee table and sat down at the far end, leaving only the space in between for me. Sit next to that? Uh-uh.

I followed Richie and tried to force my butt between him and the arm but only got halfway 'cause Richie was shoving.

"There ain't no room, pendeja," said Richie. "Go sit in the middle."

Mama gave Richie a look and after a little more pushing he finally moved over some to let me in. Soon as she had her back turned, Richie shoved me into the couch arm, digging it so deep in my ribs I could barely breathe.

While Mama poured the tea, Abuela sang with the radio in the kitchen. Sang loud and beautiful and in Spanish. I wished I could've understood it. But Spanish came all hard to me.

"My mother's not well," Pape said to El Jefe. "The music fills us all with a little hope that she will come back to us."

Hope. That's why he came to help us, the Dark One, or as they chant in Mexico City, El Jefe de Diablo, the Boss of the Devil. Pape said the people in Mexico City splashed El Jefe with prayers and holy water, chanting his name when he walked down the street. Even the priest sat with the crowds in the most famous arena in Mexico, Diablo de Ojo, with a betting ticket in one palm, the rosary in the other. Some of the people in the Circle say El Jefe killed three men in Diablo for no more than the cost of a cup of coffee. Say he did it for the crowd . . . them chanting, "Silencio, silencio, Diablo."

Mama handed the cup of iced tea to El Jefe. His arms, thick pipes popped with veins, made the smudged tattoo of a cobra coiled down his arm seem almost alive in his skin. Every time the Dark One's fist moved, the snake crushed the skull and crossbones in its mouth over and over.

Richie elbowed me to check it out like I somehow missed it and I shoved him back, making him spill his iced tea onto El Jefe's gigantic black boots.

"Richie," Mama said.

"Ay, it was Chula," he said. "Why don't you tell her something?"

"Go get your things out of your room, so you don't bother El Jefe in the morning," said Mama.

"Why not her room?" Richie asked, looking at me.

" 'Cause she said yours," said Pape.

Richie put his cup on the table. "I'm not doing it for you," said Richie to Pape.

"Hey, no more," said Mama to him. "And Chula, get ready for bed."

Richie yanked me off the couch and shoved me forward and just as I shoved back Mama stood up. Richie grinned real big and stepped back with his hands up. Then broke for the bathroom to shave, again. Even though he ain't got nothing but little fuzzy like a kitten on his face. Like nothing that girls are really into.

Richie had been in the bathroom for forever and a dozen years when I banged on the door.

"Enough already. Let me in, pendejo."

He cracked the door, his face all foamy. "The more you shave the more it grow," he said. "That's why the hair on your legs is so long."

He laughed and slammed the door in my face.

"I don't shave, cabrón."

"Then you're really in trouble," he said.

My brother's kinda stupid. Though some say it might not be true take my word on it. He was. Even though he was fourteen and useta make straight As, he flunked the eighth grade, and I let him know it every chance I got 'cause we were both in junior high at the same time and he hated that. Only I was in seventh in *accelerated classes* which meant I was supposed to be smart only it was really hard 'cause I couldn't just sit and think of other cool stuff. Like the world.

I heard the heavy footsteps of El Jefe coming from the living room and ran to my room. El Jefe's shadow clawed the hall wall before his way big body. They both slipped by my door like smoke. I stuck my head out just as he shut my brother's bedroom door at the end of the hall.

"Chula," Mama said.

I almost jumped right outta my skin.

"Why aren't you ready for bed?" she asked,

9

her rosary in one hand and a cup of hot Lipton tea in the other.

"Why do you think?" I asked.

"Just knock on the door," she said.

The bathroom was right next to Richie's room. No way was I going to stand there all alone with El Jefe only a few feet and a wooden door away.

"Ay," Mama said, grabbing my elbow. "You're being silly." She stopped outside the bathroom door. "Richie."

"What?" he asked with the water running.

"Hurry up. Your sister needs to get in there."

He opened the door. "I done say to her I was almost done."

She shook her head and went to her room. "No more trouble," she said. "I already have too many prayers to make."

Soon as she was gone he grinned and shut the door in my face.

Before I could even think to tell Richie something, a noise came from Richie's room. A dragging-scratching-squealing noise. Like finger-nails across wood across something else spooky. Whatever El Jefe could be doing in the darkness of Richie's room sent my heart beating in my throat. I tried to swallow it down but it was too big.

I beat on the bathroom door. "Come on, Richie."

"Ay, I'm almost done . . . in an hour." He laughed.

There were footsteps. Deep creaking the wood floor footsteps. How could a thing that killed for no more than the cost of a cup of coffee sleep only two doors down from me? What if he came roaring out the door right then and—

I beat on the door again.

"Please, Richie," I said.

"In a minute, pest," Richie said behind the door.

I closed my eyes, trying not to think about El Jefe. It stayed quiet inside Richie's room, so I slowly opened one eye, turning my head at the same time. A light came through the crack my brother put in the door when he got mad at Pape and slammed his metal baseball bat at it. I was in the kitchen when Richie did it and heard the smash-ba-ziNG . . . bounce all over the house. But right then, there wasn't a single sound. Nothing but the glow of light from the crack in the door. What was the beast doing in there?

I walked real careful up to the door and put my eye to the broken place. A new prayer candle glowed on the nightstand. El Jefe sat with his legs crossed Indian style, looking out the window. His hands on his knees. He'd moved Richie's bed so he could be closer to the window. I never seen anyone look like that, not up at the sky.

"What are you doing?" Richie asked.

I jumped real high 'cause the pendejo snuck up on me. I slug-bugged him in the arm.

"Ouch, puta," he said, punching me back.

Mama asked from her room, "What's going on?"

I ran to the bathroom, shut the door and locked it.

"Get to bed," she said to Richie.

I opened the medicine cabinet and pulled out my toothpaste and three bottles of pills. I shook the bottles real hard and imagined them maracas not medicine. I imagined them anything but what kept me from falling down.

2

Mama put the taquitos on the table. "Why were you spying last night?" she asked me.

I poured store-bought salsa in lumps all over my breakfast.

"Well?" she asked like I didn't hear her the first time.

"I wasn't."

"Ay, you're about to start a lie. No lying before breakfast or you'll burn in hell like Tía Josie," Mama said. "He's come here to help us. Don't go distracting him with your spying, Chula."

My real name is Esperanza. That's what Abuela says. Mama and Pape changed their mind when Mama's baby sister Tía Josie had a girl just two days before me and named her Esperanza. They hated Tía Josie more than they hated gringos who smiled back at us when they were really thinking, "Filthy Mexican. Go back to your country."

"Like we're already in our freakin' country, pendejos," Richie would say when it came up.

Things woulda been different if they stuck with my real name instead of naming me Chula 'cause Chula means pretty and there ain't nothing pretty about me now. That much Mama made sure I knew. Especially with the darkening scar on the side of my head, standing out like some bratty kid in church.

"Do you hear me, Chula?" asked Mama.

"Yes . . . ," I said, rolling my eyes.

"Don't roll your eyes at me," she said. "And where's your brother?"

"I don't know. Where he *always* is."

Mama shouted down the hall, "Richie! Get out of that shower or you're going to pay that bill this month."

14

El Jefe clopped in, his feet like horse hooves. My eyes hit my plate as he pulled out a chair, right next to me. Mama sat down three potato and egg taquitos so full they were falling out of the tortillas. Even the eggs and potatoes were trying to get away from him.

"Mi'jo, do you want something special?" Mama asked him.

He rolled his head into a no, drowning the inside of his taquitos in Mama's homemade salsa. And man, was that stuff hot!

She put a hand on his back and said, "We're very grateful for you coming. We want you to have whatever you want."

He nodded, picking up one of those enormous taquitos that looked like a pencil in his gigantic paws.

Touching his back and smiling seemed like a real chore for her. Maybe she was scared of him too. He looked at me and I squirmed around in my seat. As long as he wasn't eating Mexican girls for breakfast, I figured I was fine.

I walked to school behind Richie every day. Mama made him go with me even though I was already twelve and way too old to be walking with my dumb brother. But last year, a Mexican girl walking to high school got taken by some gringos outside the Circle and Mama ain't been good about letting me go nowhere alone since.

"You're too close," said Richie all loud 'cause he couldn't hear himself.

He was jamming to his hot MP3 player that he'd been hiding from Pape for weeks. And it wasn't hot like cool, it was hot like five-finger discount 'cause there was no way he coulda bought something like that. We ain't had nothing for extra since he got busted at the Playground.

I kicked broken beer-bottle glass off smeared hopscotch squares. I wondered what it would be like to draw them in with fat pieces of colored chalk like kids do in Squaretown instead of with rocks. We turned the corner and Richie grabbed a stick and ran, thumping it against the chain fences, barking. Dogs jumped from their porches or wherever they were, barking like crazy. They got as far up to the fences as their faces would go. Snarling and growling and Richie snarled and growled back.

"You're so stupid," I said.

"Shut up, fatty."

I shoved him and he fake-hit me just to see me flinch.

"*Bac! Bac bac bac!* My sister the chicken. Pobrecita."

He flung the stick into one of the yards, jacked up the volume and walked off.

Richie's dumb-head friends Raul and Paul, twins with dimples and strange warts, sat on the back of a bus stop bench waiting for us. A slap-slide shake with Richie and they all kept walking like I wasn't even there.

We were almost outta the Circle when Freddy Cortez shouted, "Hey Richie," from across the street.

Freddy ran the Dark Skins and he was the darkest of all of them. He was sixteen and had big arms and small ears and a nose like a rat. Freddy had already been in jail and Richie thought that was all cool 'cause Freddy done time and got out and they didn't break him. No way did those gringos break Freddy Cortez.

Freddy was standing outside Alvarado's Bakery with a couple of other Dark Skins. He waved to Richie, and Richie like some kinda good dog jogged across the street with Raul and Paul behind him like always.

"We're gonna be late," I yelled at Richie.

"Just stay there, Chula."

Freddy had it easy getting guys to do what he wanted in the Circle, which wasn't much since his big brother and a bunch of the older Dark Skins got locked up over the summer for something like seven years. But they still followed him 'cause besides being broke and riding your bike if you got one, there wasn't nothing to do. And 'cause of that stupid home ink they all had on their hands.

The guys did a macho-macho show-off handshake as Freddy led them behind the bakery where I couldn't see.

There wasn't nowhere to sit that I wouldn't get all dirty so I just stood there. Stood there looking at the Circle, which was mostly Mexican with a couple of blacks and whites squished in on one edge. Abuela useta say when I was little, if you could see the neighborhood from up high, all the buildings made up a circle. That it was a gift to live somewhere so magical. To live somewhere that always meets itself.

It didn't seem so magical with houses all on

top of each other. Most of them with their roofs all sagging, door gates and windows with thick bars. The Projects full of babies crying and people fighting and it always smelled of stinky diapers and beer. The only thing that seemed magical in the Circle was that everybody just kept going round and round chasing their damn tails 'cause they couldn't get out, not even the smart ones. Like Mama's baby sister Tía Josie. She was a class smart girl with a scholarship to some Ivory school and there she goes sleeping with some easy boy with blue eyes and pale skin and BAM! She got seeds in her belly. Nine months later, one of them seeds, it was Esperanza, the most beautiful girl in the Circle. Ask anyone, they'd tell you. Anyone but Mama. It didn't matter none to her 'cause Tía Josie got swollen by a gringo. Nobody in my family 'cept Abuela was forgiving of that but "Abuela isn't right in the head," Mama would say every time I tried to bring up Tía.

Even after Esperanza died when she was just ten, Mama couldn't forgive Tía Josie and for what I didn't even know. Seeds? And every day we walked past Tía's tiny house on the way to school. It was so quiet from the street. And every day I just wanted to tell Richie to stop walking by so we could go say her something. Anything. We didn't even go to the funeral or send flowers or nothing. That seemed wrong.

They all came from behind the bakery only Richie was carrying a shiny silver cell phone. He gave Freddy a cool handshake and crossed the street showing it off to the twins. Freddy saw me standing there and kicked his head back at me. I caught up with Richie, who was already leaving me behind.

"What's that for?" I asked, looking at his phone.

"Don't worry about it," said Richie.

Richie passed the phone to Raul and Paul who made it ring like ten different ways.

"Man, you can download all kinds of ringers," said Raul.

Richie snatched the phone back. "You ain't downloading nothing on here 'cept a picture of your cousin . . . en mi cama."

"Man, don't be talking about my cousin," said Raul.

I walked faster until I could step right on top of the back of his sneakers and really not meaning to, did.

"Walk slower," he said.

I slowed down but he was taking pictures with the phone and showing it to those dumb-heads so I picked up the pace again and was like two people behind him when he turned around and shoved me, only when I fell I saw he didn't think I would. Paul and Raul laughed. Richie felt bad but I felt even worse 'cause I landed in mud. He tried to help me up and I pushed him away.

"Well, don't walk so close next time, okay?" he snapped.

He headed off with his cackling dumb-heads. I didn't see how we could be blood 'cause I'd never be as stupid as him. I'd never fail the eighth grade.

3

i peeled through the crowded junior high halls hating every second of it. Junior high is like the biggest hell on earth with the exception of catechism. It was the first time you got out of the Circle to go to school and what's the point 'cause the Squaretown kids make sure you know you don't belong. Squaretown, it was about eight blocks from where we lived and those kids living there ain't nothing like us. They came in all colors but smelled like cable TV, camera phones, expensive sneakers, JNCO jeans and all the CDs you want. Being a Square means you're always asked questions in class first and you never have to stand at the back of the line at lunch. Most of all, and the thing Circles never forget, being a Square meant you'd never have to wish for nothing 'cause you already got everything or the chances for it.

I spotted Mary Alice and Jo waiting at my locker. They were my best friends, my only friends, and they ain't Squares even though Mary Alice started that way before her dad quit her mom when she was six and they had to move outta Squaretown to the Circle. We treated her all the same even though she was part Square.

"¿Qué pasó, Mexican?" said Jo with a secret palm-slide-snap shake.

"Nada, nada," I said.

"Why you all dirty?" asked Jo.

"I fell."

My friends looked nervous.

"Stop looking at me all scared," I said to them.

I fell a lot right after the accident. I useta be a little kinda popular before the Flashes started at the end of sixth grade. It scared most kids and their parents were all mean about it. They'd back away from me like some kind of monster. I stayed in the house almost all summer hoping that everybody would just forget about it. But the first week of seventh grade I Flashed right there at my locker between first and second period. It was all kinds of horrible. 'Cause it was one thing for the Squares to treat me all weird. They didn't like me 'cause I was a Circle anyways. But it was worse in the Circle I guess 'cause nothing makes you feel worse than the people who are like you being afraid of you. If Mama wasn't pushing me out the door making my dumb-head brother drag me along, no way would I've come back to school.

"So did he come before you left this morning?" asked Mary Alice.

I rolled the combination to my lock. I never could remember numbers anymore. There was so much freaking–

"Move, Mexican," Jo said, shoving me to the side to get to my locker.

"So did he?" Mary Alice asked.

"Yeah," I said to Mary Alice. "He came last night."

Jo popped open the locker. "Chula . . . ," said Jo, holding her nose.

My lunch from two days ago was the first thing we caught a whiff of.

"Ay, all right," I said. "I thought I was gonna eat it yesterday."

"So tell us about him," said Mary Alice. "Is he the way people talk about him?"

"Yeah, and does he eat from a bowl like a dog?" Jo asked. "Claw at his food? Drool and snarl with teeth sharp like switchblades?"

"He's quiet," I said.

That didn't impress either of them. They wanted to hear some gory horrific story of the beast with one eye and arms like shadows and fists like pit bulls. They wanted to hear he stomped into the house like an unchained roaring animal and broke the Virgin that was on the mantle and made Jesus weep in the bathroom. They wanted to hear that the devil himself slept in a chair beside his bed smoking Luckys and drinking sangria. They wanted to hear that he snored so loud the roof of the house came up just a little. Just enough for the smell of stale garbage from across the street to sweep in. They wanted to hear that he was not just any old monster but the Cacooey himself, the most feared monster of all.

But the only thing I could think of with Jo and Mary Alice standing there was that he was quiet. Really quiet and sort of calm staring out Richie's bedroom window.

"Chula?" said Mary Alice, touching my arm lightly.

They thought maybe I was gonna Flash only I wasn't.

"I don't know, okay?" I said. "He came in like really late and they sent us to bed. Richie had to sleep on the pullout in the living room."

"You saw him, right?" asked Jo.

"Well, yeah. I ain't blind."

"Then?" Mary Alice asked.

"Then nothing," I said, looking at the two of them. "I went to bed."

I slammed the locker shut.

"Just tell me this," said Jo, leaning in close. "Do you think he can win?"

I looked at Mary Alice who swished her lips to the side like when she wanted to ask too but didn't want to be rude or something.

"I don't know how he could lose," I said.

Jo's lips parted in a sinister grin. She hooked her arm around my neck.

"Squaretown is going down," said Jo. "And if he's as good as Li'l Pete's been talking him up, then your family will make a lotta cha-ching the next couple of weeks."

"What are you doing talking to Freddy's guys?" I asked.

"Pues, nothing. I just bump into him. Relax, Chula. I ain't no gangbanger."

As we headed off to homeroom, I saw Richie with a couple of Mexicans. They ran with Freddy too and, like Richie, had flunked out. Some of them at least twice. How stupid was that?

Ring . . . !

Jo shoved Mary Alice and me inside the door of Mr. Maskin's homeroom/algebra class. Mr. Maskin gave us a glance over his shoulder as he wrote on the chalkboard. The class snickered their mostly pale faces.

"Please pass your homework forward," said Mr. Maskin.

I flipped open my folder and realized I left my homework at home. Man . . . not again.

I looked over at Ross the Floss staring out the window only the blinds were shut and you couldn't see nothing but in the cracks. He was the Floss 'cause he was obsessed with his new teeth, the teeth without braces. Actually, he had an okay smile for a gringo but I'd never tell Jo or Mary Alice that.

"Has everyone handed in their homework?" asked Mr. Maskin.

I didn't look up off my desk.

"Okay. Clear your desks. Pencils only."

We had to take two quizzes a week in algebra. Which was two separate times for me to fail in a week. Mr. Maskin was the master of hard tests. Before we took a quiz, he handed back the one most of us failed two days earlier. I think it was to make sure our concentration was off.

Mr. Maskin toured the rows of silent kids in his marching band style with these quick exact moves, calling out names. Flipping our tests FACE UP so that anyone around could lean over and see how stupid you were. Kids quit looking at my tests before the end of September.

Mr. Maskin slapped my test facedown, moving to a desk three back without so much as a glance at me. I imagined a rattlesnake on the other side of the paper. I fingered the edge before flippin' it over. It said at the top in bright teacher-pen red

SEE ME AFTER CLASS
F

I'd never got a See Me After Class F. This was a new kinda grade. My stomach flip-flopped. A See Me After Class F had to be the worst kind of F. The kind Mama would definitely ground me for my entire life or at least until after Mary Alice's party weekend after next. Either way, it was going to be way too long.

After class, I stood kind of nervous in front of Mr. Maskin's desk as the other kids piled out. Jo and Mary Alice waited for me at the door.

"Go on to class," Mr. Maskin said to them. "Go on."

They peeled off, leaving me totally in trouble.

"Where's your homework?" he asked me.

I shrugged.

"Okay, I'll make this quick, Chew-lah."

I hated it when they couldn't get my name right. Just don't even try if you can't say it right.

"You are not doing well in this class. Your test

29

scores suggested you could handle this level of complexity. I've tried to talk to you about . . ."

I just sort of drowned him out. It was the same thing all my teachers were telling me lately. The usual "Chula, you're not focused." Or "Chula, is it your father? We know about the accident." Or the most often was "The episodes might be distracting you too much."

Since the accident, I drifted more. The doctors said it was common for a while even with the medication. That it would get better, but what was better? How worse was I? Why did they keep expecting—

"So I wanted you to know that I called your mother—"

I was startled back to what he was saying. "What?" I asked.

"I didn't know what else to do. It's the middle of October and I can't have you taking up a seat that a hardworking, determined young man or woman could be using. These kids want to go places, Chew-lah. Do you want to go places?"

I looked at him and couldn't help the knives I flung at him. Did he know where I lived?

"If you don't improve," said Mr. Maskin,

"we'll have to put you in lower-level classes. Possibly Special Needs if that doesn't work out."

"With the droopy eyes?" I asked, all shocked.

"Do you understand what I'm saying?"

"I ain't no retard," I said.

"We have to have someone in your desk who wants to learn."

"Someone white?" I asked.

"Someone who can do the work."

I ain't no retard.

4

fifth-period lunch: pill-popping at the nurse's office. Had to wait for Ross the Floss to get his breathing treatment. Even if he was the handsomest gringo in school he couldn't run a half a block without wheezing and falling down.

He came from behind the curtain and looked real tired. "Hey, Chula," Ross the Floss said.

I acted like I couldn't even see him. He waited for what felt like forever, then walked away.

The school nurse had my usual. One pink and a blue. Little white cup. Slam. Done!

Lunch was gross as usual. I was late and got

cold hamburger surprise, french fries and magic brownies. The surprise was that I gotta eat it for the second day in a row and the magic was it always ran through me before seventh period. Jo and Mary Alice were already sitting in Tan Land. That's where Mexicans from the Circle sat. It was clear across the cafeteria from the Squares and especially from Royal Rich. See, I know how they say in history books all that stuff about America being a melting pot. The only thing melting in our lunchroom was our skin 'cause the air conditioner broke and in October it was still like eighty-five freaking degrees.

The geeks and freaks sat closest to the food in Brain Reign in case they wanted seconds, and they usually did. Then there was the sk8ters, perm outs, preppies, sluppies (sloppy yuppies), gangstas, tough guys, cool clique, Royal Rich and of course Tan Land/poor. Tan Land was the worst section 'cause almost all of us got free food and everybody knew it 'cause of the pink lunch card that gets hole-punched.

"Hey Chula," said Mary Alice.

"Hey." I sat my tray down across from Jo who looked really pissed.

"I'll be right back," said Jo.

"What's up?" I asked Mary Alice.

"You know," she said, looking over at Royal Rich. "Before you got here Carla and Mitzy walked by and started picking at her."

"What did Jo do?"

"Nothing. Principal Shannon was standing by the door. They just want to get her suspended."

Jo slid back into her seat with two cartons of chocolate milk. Her eyes fixed on Carla's table as she dug her fingers into the carton mouth.

"What makes them so better?" asked Jo. "Look at that."

Mary Alice stared at her tray. I turned around in my seat to Royal Rich and saw Carla and Mitzy. Eighth graders. Best friends since the crib.

"I don't know what makes them better," I said, almost gagging on my soggy burger. "Money, I guess."

"You know what," said Jo. "I think they're sheep. All of them."

One thing I respected about Jo, she hated the way things were and there was no telling her why they were anymore 'cause she didn't care about the why. She just thought it was wrong. She could run for student council president and be the best ever if she stopped wearing baggies and put on a dress and Keds. She'd win by a landslide but you couldn't tell Jo that. No way. She wouldn't change. Just like when Carla threw a volleyball at the back of my head in seventh-period PE a coupla weeks into school. Jo sprung off the bench and landed Carla flat on her back in one punch. Ouch! We all got wall-sits and a half a dozen other stupid punishments. Carla knew I'd scrambled my eggs up there and threw that ball at me anyways. If that ain't mean, I don't know what is. But when I go home and tell Pape he told me what he always does: "There's always a better way than fighting."

So why he sent for El Jefe I couldn't understand, but I didn't say him nothing when he told us that he did. Even if Richie didn't believe it, Pape always had a way, at least before the accident, of making things right. I just wanted to believe he still could.

"Sheep," Jo said. *"Baaahhhhhh . . . "*

Mary Alice snorted and chocolate milk came out her nose. Jo and me laughed.

"It's not funny," said Mary Alice. "Quit laughing."

"Ay, relax Mary Alice," said Jo. "It really is funny."

* * *

35

After school, Jo and Mary Alice walked home with me 'cause Richie ran off with the Dark Skins. Jo and me mostly did a lot of nodding 'cause Mary Alice rolled on and on about her party the next weekend. It sounded real good and real expensive but her mother was always doing that . . . trying to spend more than they got. Mama said, "That's just how some people get by, Chula. Even if it doesn't make any sense you have to let them be who they are."

Mary Alice was turning thirteen which isn't a big year for being Mexican like fifteen but her mother was making it that way. She worked two jobs and layawayed a lotta stuff to give her this Richie-Rich birthday party that they couldn't afford, no way.

"Can you believe she's really getting Danny D to deejay," said Mary Alice, "from Power 95? And we're taking all the furniture out of the living room for dancing. Oh, and she's getting this two-layered cake that's as big as . . ." Mary Alice held out her arms as far as they'd stretch. "Maybe even bigger than that. She says she wants it to be the best birthday I ever had. Everyone's coming. I wonder what kind of gifts I'll get. OH, my GOD!

Do you think I'll get a CD player? That would be so great. Then you could all come over after school and listen to La Mafia and Cumbo Kings and Justin Timberlake and . . ."

Mary Alice didn't have a lot of good birthdays. Usually her dad called a couple of weeks before and made a promise that he'd pick her up and take her somewhere really nice. He never showed and every year she got less excited around her birthday. That day was the first time that I'd seen her smile about it in like four years.

"Hey, Chula, forgot to tell you who I seen in Squaretown last night," said Jo. "Your tía."

"Tía Josie?" I asked.

"Yeah, she's got a job at this real nice store in the mall. Expensive clothes for tiny twits like Carla and Mitzy."

"Couldn't have been Tía. Mama said she just sits around the house all day. That she ain't doing nothing."

"Your mama don't even talk to her. What does she know?" asked Jo.

We stopped outside the lopsided fence Pape was gonna fix. I wanted them to come in but Mama won't have Jo in her house.

"She's just a few loose dates from seeds, Chula. I know that kind of girl," Mama said to me whenever I asked if Jo could come over.

But Mama didn't know the kind of girl Jo was and I'm not sure Jo did either.

"We'll see you tomorrow," Mary Alice said.

They headed off down the street. "Hey, Chula," shouted Jo. "Watch out for the Cacooey. Ooooo. . ."

I thought about going somewhere else but then what? Get caught coming home after dark by El Jefe? No way. I closed the gate and saw Abuela slowly rocking on the porch swing. The chains creaked and squeaked like little angry mice. Abuela's shriveled feet and drawn-in toes scraped the floor. She was a dancer when she was young. The most beautiful untouched flower in Mexico City. I could still see it in her cloudy dusty eyes even then. There was something in the way she always smiled through the pain of her dead-nerved feet and the sadness of Abuelo dying so young.

I felt sad for her. Sad that she couldn't remember Abuelo's name anymore. That the colors and spices that she useta sprinkle in her stories were frozen behind her smiling daydreams and humming of songs I'd never heard.

Abuela blinked. Yawned so wide all her saggy skin stretched tight across her face.

"Chulita," said Abuela. "What time is it?"

"I don't know," I said. "I just come home from school."

"Sit with me," she said, patting her hand on the swing.

I sat next to her and she picked up my hand, squeezing it as hard as she could.

"How do you like school?" she asked me.

I thought of telling her the truth. Telling her how I hated going to that Squaretown school every day. And how Richie wasn't like he useta be and I didn't know how to get along with him no more. I thought of telling her how much Mama missed her and how much she hated me.

But then I remembered how little she would remember and telling the truth seemed wasted on her.

"It's good, Abuela," I said. "I'm popular and I got first chair in band last week and Richie likes high school."

"That's so good, mi'jita," said Abuela.

She raised her arms to the ceiling stretching and dropped them like rain at her side.

"Only you're lying," said Abuela. "I can see

the sadness in your eyes, mi'jita. Eyes do not lie. You know that."

"Chula," Mama said from the screen door.

Abuela turned to Mama and for a moment Mama lit up.

"Abuela," said Mama. "Did Chula wake you?"

"No," said Abuela, standing. "I was thinking of Mexico and then I saw Chula and could only think of Texas."

"Are you hungry?" asked Mama.

"No, Elena," said Abuela, pulling the screen door open. "I am too tired to eat. Chula, I'm glad to hear you like school."

She disappeared in the house. Mama turned back to me.

"Why are you dirty?" she asked.

"I fell," I said. "And no, not like that. I just tripped."

"You tripped and fell backwards. Bueno. At least you're lying after breakfast. Where's Richie?"

I knew exactly where Richie was. The Playground with the rest of the Dark Skins. Probably smoking pot and plotting another robbery of the convenient store at the end of the street. Only come robbery time he'd say he got grounded or that something happened and he'd help them come up with something later. They never really did nothing but stupid stuff like spray-paint the side of the Catholic church and curse a lot at people who usually couldn't hear them.

"I don't know," I said to Mama. "He was in a hurry."

She pushed the door open for me.

"I'm gonna beat that boy to heaven when he comes home. You can't be walking from school by yourself."

"Mama, I'm twelve," I said. "I'm nearly grown up already."

"When you get your period, you're still not grown—"

"Mama, gross—"

"When your breasts swell, you're still not grown. And most of all, when you're still in my house you're not grown. ¿Comprende?"

She always had to remind me that even though I was almost as tall as her, I'd probably never be taller in the ways it really counted.

"Put your books down and help me with dinner."

"I got homework."

"After dinner," she said. "Andale."

I smacked my books down on the kitchen table and picked up the rolling pin.

"Ay, wash your hands," said Mama. "No wonder this gringo's calling me from the school about you," said Mama.

I let the water run over my hands an extralong time.

"Well?" she asked.

"I don't know," I said, wiping my hands on a dishrag. I started rolling out tortillas on the counter.

"He wants me to come in and talk with all your teachers and the principal about pulling you out of those classes."

"I'm not flat brained, Mama."

She dropped a tortilla on the stove. "I know you're not," she said.

"Did you tell him? Did you tell him not to?"

She shuffled the tortilla.

"Mama?"

"I listened to him, Chula. What do you want me to say? I mean maybe it is better for a while that you not take those hard classes."

"What?"

"You don't want to be like Richie. God help us, I don't want you to be like Richie. Don't look at me like that, Chula. Give me the tortilla."

I peeled the tortilla off the counter and dropped it on the skillet.

"It's been a hard year and you know it," she said. "With Pape, with–" And she looked at me like she always did when she had to stop herself from saying it.

She still couldn't say it. Say what happened. And I didn't want to blame her but I did. She wouldn't even hold me no more.

The back door slammed shut and in rolled Richie, filthy as a pig. He made for the cabinet and the half a bag of Cool Ranch Doritos, my favorite.

"No, sir. You're lucky I let you eat dinner. I told you to walk your sister home."

I smiled all big teeth at him. He swatted at my head and I ducked.

"Enough. Richie, shoes off and straight to the shower. Then go down the street to the Hinojosas' and pick up the things El Jefe needs to train."

"Ay, all right already," he said, digging out a handful of chips.

I reached for the bag and he jerked it away.

"Cut it out," I said.

He held the chips over my head. I jumped to grab them and the dumb-head yanked them away. Soon as I quit trying he threw the bag at me and the chips spilt all over the floor.

"Thanks a lot, flunkie," I said.

"Shut up, twitchie."

"Richie, ahora vaya," Mama snapped.

He pulled off his shoes and put them at the back door while I picked up the chips and dumped them in the garbage.

"Chula, I didn't tell him anything except to give you more time," said Mama. "You'll just have to try better or you know where you'll end up."

"End up where?" asked Richie.

"Nowhere," I said.

I made a silent prayer that she wouldn't tell him anything. If word got to Richie that they wanted to pull me outta *accelerated*, I'd never live it down. It would be like the time I couldn't hold it and peed at the grocery store when I was five. To this day, he goes on every time we're in aisle four, "Is that water I hear? Warm, warm water."

Maybe he wasn't my real brother. Maybe a coyote brung him over when he was still little and couldn't sell him to a gringo family and he was left at our doorstep. Mama useta be such a soft heart that she couldn't turn him over to Immigration and kept him. Maybe he wasn't just an illegal alien but an alien altogether. That would explain why he was the only one who ate and talked with his food in his mouth.

"What did she do this time?" Richie asked.

"No more," said Mama. "Shower now before I take a belt to you."

"I'm too old," said Richie.

"You think?" And her expression sent him to the shower.

I'd never been so pleased with her in my whole entire life.

5

At dinner, El Jefe sat real quiet with a few spoon-fuls of peas, frijoles, and carne guisada on his plate. A horseshoe of a tortilla and a tall glass of milk in each paw. The only reason we weren't strangled by how quiet it was, was 'cause Abuela sang to herself in Spanish. Richie sat across from me staring at El Jefe as he wiped up the gravy with a crumpled tortilla. Me, I just picked at my food 'cause carne guisada looks like dog puke to me and if I sat there picking long enough Mama got frustrated and sent me to my room.

"Sorry I'm late," shouted Tío Tony from the back door in the kitchen.

"Tony, I didn't know you were coming for dinner," said Mama.

"I invited him," said Pape. "He's going to work with El Jefe after."

Mama was halfway outta her chair when Tío Tony, Pape's brother, came in wiping his wet hands on his blue jeans.

"I'll get you a plate," said Mama to Tío Tony.

"Buenos noches, Chulita," he said, kissing the top of my head.

His hair was wet from showering but no matter how much soap he used, Tío Tony's skin always smelled of motor oil and grease.

He knelt beside Abuela and kissed her lightly on the cheek. "¿Cómo estás, Mama?"

She said nothing and we all looked away. All of us but El Jefe, who watched them with the softest eyes. Tío Tony caught El Jefe's stare and leaned over the table holding his hand out to him. El Jefe shook Tío's hand and immediately dropped his eyes to his plate.

"Good trip?" Tío asked.

He nodded.

"What's up, Tío?" said Richie all macho-macho.

Tío Tony grinned, scooting up next to me. "Nothing but hard honest work, Richie. How about you?"

"Pues, you know."

"He spent all of last week in In-School Suspension," said Pape. "What was it?"

"Hector," said Mama.

"Ditching PE?" Pape asked Richie.

Mama set a plate and a gigantic glass of iced tea in front of Tío Tony.

"Whatever," said Richie.

"Gracias, Elena," said Tío Tony.

Richie just sat there running his fingers down his sweaty iced tea.

"You know Richie, you could come down to the garage after school. We're always looking for an extra hand."

"Your Tío's talking to you," said Pape.

"What are people saying about the fight?" asked Mama, hoping to smother the fire between Pape and Richie.

"The bets are high. Really high," said Tío Tony, dumping carne guisada onto a tortilla.

"Even the coconuts in Squaretown are laying some fat cash on this one."

Tío Tony's favorite word for a Mexican that had more than us was coconut. Brown on the outside, white on the inside. He figured if they had more than us they musta sold out.

With a mouth full of food and a gulp of tea, Tío Tony said, "You decided how much you're going to lay down, Hector?"

"Three thousand," said Pape.

"What?" asked Mama.

"El Jefe can beat this boy, Elena," said Pape.

"Yes, fine. Then let him win this week and next week, but to bet everything that we have, Hector? It's insane." She said the last part to herself only we all somehow heard.

"Elena, Golden Gloves is four to one," said Tío Tony. "That means for every thousand dollars you put down you make four more when El Jefe wins."

"And how much are you betting, Tony?"

"All the guys at the garage are making one bet. A thousand five hundred," said Tío Tony.

Mama shook her head at her plate.

Pape knew nothing of boxing and even less

about betting. He wasn't like Tío Tony or any dozen other relatives who lived by the odds of the weekly prizefights. He didn't even play Lotto Texas. Sometimes Pape and me would go in the Kwick Stop and people would be lined up for forever and ten days for one of them tickets. I seen them spend like twenty dollars and for what? A chance? A chance in a million? Pape never saw the point in chance like that. "Chance is too risky," he'd say. "You have to invest in what is solid, what is sure."

For him that had become El Jefe, the most renowned prizefighter in all of Mexico. That was for sure. Guaranteed. El Jefe never lost a fight. Not once. But neither had Golden Gloves and Mama knew it and there Pape was saying to us that he'd bet the last of our money on a man who didn't speak. Maybe he couldn't. Maybe he had no words. Just growls and barks and howls. Maybe if he opened his mouth to do anything but that he could only speak the words of death. Whatever words that would be 'cause I didn't know.

"We went to watch him train today," Pape said. "He's thick but small. Very fast. Arms like pistons but . . . "

Mama didn't lift her eyes off her plate and good for Pape 'cause I think she might've knocked him outta his chair just with her look.

"Elena, this Golden Gloves, he's very showy," said Pape.

"It's true," said Tío Tony. "The kid's real full of himself. I seen him fight two weeks ago against Omar Hinojosa. Golden Gloves danced around acting like some kind of clown. He wasn't fighting smart. He was fighting to look smart."

"Who won?" asked Mama.

"That's not the point," said Pape.

"You want to bet three thousand of our dollars and I can't ask?"

"Golden Gloves," said Tío Tony. "But that doesn't mean anything. I bet you anything Omar threw that fight. El Jefe won't."

El Jefe reached across the table and Richie and I both went back as far as we could in our chairs. Both our backs like boards. El Jefe lifted the lid off the tortilla warmer and pulled out a steaming tortilla and sat back down.

Richie cocked his head back acting like he wasn't just as scared as me when that Cyclops got up, only he was. Faker.

"We're all really glad that you're here. All of us," Pape said to El Jefe.

Mama stretched into a forced smile. El Jefe didn't look at her but at me, and my heart did that in-my-throat thing like when I rode the Tilt-A-Whirl at the cheap carnival that came to town once a year. The kind that's all squeaky and wobbles like it could spin off at any second and you know it. That's how it felt inside me.

"This guy's a champion, El Jefe," said Richie. "Never lost a fight. A lot of gringos say he'll go pro."

El Jefe dropped his attention back to his plate.

"Chula," said Mama. "Ay dios mio, enough picking at your dinner. Are you going to eat?"

I shook my head. She dropped her head in her palm.

"Leave, go," she said.

I got up from the table and dumped my taquito in the trash. I was almost out of the kitchen when she asked, "Chula, where are you going?"

"To my room."

"No mam," said Mama. "You don't want to eat, you can do the dishes."

"I done did 'em last night."

Richie grinned 'cause he knew it was his turn.

"I'm serious," said Mama. "Start with the skillets. We'll be done soon."

I stomped around the kitchen banging the dishes in the sink.

"Stop fooling around in there," shouted Mama.

Richie came in rubbing his belly and holding out his plate.

"What?" I said. "Put it down."

He got in real close as he set the plate on the counter and BELCHED in my ear.

"Ay, Mama . . ."

"Richie, whatever you're doing stop it," she shouted from the dining room.

"You're such a crybaby, Chula."

"Shut up."

"You know . . ." Richie lowered his voice. "El Jefe fought a ring of rabid dogs tall as small horses and the size of bears and still won."

"Whatever," I said, dunking a skillet.

"It's true. Pues. You see how scarred up his skin is. It was from those dogs sinking their poisoned teeth into his skin. Tío Tony says that the meanest of those dogs chewed El Jefe's eye right out. That if you lifted the patch you'd see the dog's teeth marks and the color of death."

I heaved out a way heavy sigh. "Right. That's

how come he's alive? Nobody lives through rabies, pendejo."

"He's a-mmune," said Richie.

"A what?" I asked.

"A-mmune. Geez, and you're in accelerated classes?"

I flung water at him.

"I would just make sure to lock your door at night," Richie said. "Tío Tony says El Jefe has some of that poison in his veins. If he finds you in the dark . . ." Richie leapt at me growling, chomping his teeth. Then busted out laughing.

"Pendejo," I said pushing him back.

"I don't know why you keep trying to speak Spanish. You don't even know what pendejo means."

"Mama!" I shouted.

"Richie," she said from the dining room.

"Ay, I wasn't doing her nothing," he said to her still looking at me.

He started walking off, then popped back at me growling and left.

Pendejo.

After me doing dishes, again, we all sat around and watched Abuela's favorite telenovela even though she fell asleep right after it started. All of us but El Jefe, who was in the basement beating bags of potatoes and sacks of dirt. I imagined his snarling fists bruising and crushing the potatoes and that if they could they'd be crying all night about the beating they just got.

smaCK-THud! smaCK-THud

BAM BAM BAM!

bounced against the ceiling of the basement, the floor of the living room. Every once in a while, there was this louder more angry sound, this like howl that ripped up through the cracks in the floor. I kept thinking about what Richie said in the kitchen. What if there was poison in El Jefe's veins? Like a cottonmouth or a rattlesnake. I imagined slobber oozing from El Jefe's strong alligator jaw. His teeth and eyes a shallow white glow from the one lightbulb hanging over the washer. I looked at Richie on the couch. When he wasn't looking, I drew my legs in on the rug to stay off the cracks. Just in case some of that poison might come through.

"Pape, can we *please* watch something else?" I asked.

"You just don't like it because it's in Spanish," said Richie.

"Shut up," I said back.

"Chula," said Pape. "We watch it because we have to be respectful of adults." He looked at Abuela. "They've earned it."

He missed her. We all missed her. Even Richie probably. Abuela's mind was in the winds and clouds that none of us could see and came back to us less and less. She useta get up every morning at five-thirty and make us these huge Mexican breakfasts. We'd wake up to the smell of cinnamon frijoles, fried apples and cherries, roasted corn, papas con huevos, fresh flour tortillas, tomatoes, and chilies, and shredded cheese. The table would look like a mosaic of paintings. Just like the ones we study about in school. All these little bright colors making up one picture. That's what Abuela would do. She'd make the picture of our family on that table every morning. After Abuela got sick, Mama mostly bought tortillas packed in smelly plastic from the HEB grocery. We ate generic cornflakes with 1% milk and our taste buds gagged when we swallowed.

I got up off the floor 'cause it was starting to make my stomach hurt feeling the noise from the basement. I tried to sit on the couch only Richie was hogging it and nudged me all hard with his stinky feet to move. I plopped on the hard footstool close to Pape wishing I'd be sent to bed or anywhere but there. There with the creature below me and nothing but Spanish in my ears.

Richie peeled back the curtain behind the couch. He was waiting for something to happen outside the window, some kind of stupid trouble.

"Whatcha looking at?" I asked him knowing he'd get it from Pape.

Pape looked over at Richie. "Richie, go do your homework in the kitchen," Pape said.

When Pape busted his back, Richie tried to stay right bagging groceries in Squaretown. But then some white lady went off talking about how she felt so sorry for him like those kids on TV. The ones some gringo asked people to send like a dollar a day to. He quit right then and started running with Freddy and the Dark Skins. That's when everyone in the Circle started callin' Richie "Slinger" 'cause he sling so much drugs without breaking a sweat. He bought us the new toaster oven, the good groceries you can't get with the welfare Lone Star Card and even the TV we watched. But he got caught at the Playground by some gringo and a coconut from Squaretown. 'Cause Mama got a real good lawyer named Ralph something who's Tío Tony's neighbor's nephew, Richie just ended up with like a thousand hours of community service picking up trash and stupid stuff like that.

"Don't just sit there. You heard me," said Pape.

"I ain't got no homework," said Richie.

His words came out with these yellow outlines that said LIES in flashing lights.

"You're not going out tonight," said Pape. "Not on a school night, flunkie."

Mama turned up the volume on the TV. Richie stood up in a wide-legged stance and tipped back his dark neck.

"Whatcha gonna do to keep me here, jefe?" said Richie to Pape.

Mama turned up the volume even louder. Both Richie and Pape steamed and boiled like a pot of water someone forgot to turn off.

"Sit down and watch the show," said Pape.

Richie glared like he had hated Pape his whole life only it was just the last few years. We all knew Pape had a problem with Coors Light and

Jack Daniel's. They were almost common names like when you talk about your neighbors or really close friends. We all knew it was hard for Pape. His days with all those Squares and their racist jokes. And with Abuela getting farther and farther from us. His heart was breaking. It really was, I swear it.

But it bothered Richie when Pape slurred through dinner or knocked over things. I thought it was funny most of the time really, and told Richie he was being too sensitive-like and he'd just make for the door or disappear in his room till we almost forgot he'd even come home.

I guess I didn't know how bad Pape was until the day he picked me up from band practice. I could smell the whiskey like it was swimming down my throat and splashing into my belly full of potato chips and Coke. I never buckled my seat belt but that time I did 'cause something told me he was too drunk. We pulled away from the band hall. We were going, I don't know where. I remember I buckled the seat belt. That's what I told them in the hospital when they kept asking my name. I said, "I buckled it. I buckled it."

I didn't know what was going on and I didn't

want Pape to get in trouble. And my arm was broken and my leg was broken and my head was hurting like crazy and the gringo doctor kept saying, "Can you tell me your name?"

"Esperanza," I said. "My name is Esperanza. . . . "

It all gets fuzzy and sharp and—

"Sit down, boy," said Pape to Richie.

Richie didn't move. "Make me, loose legs. You ain't a man anymore. You weren't before—"

And Mama shot out of her rocking chair and in one fiery move slapped Richie across the face. My mouth dropped right open.

"Don't ever disrespect your father like that again," said Mama. "And don't think you can look at me the way you've looked at him for the last eight months. Now do homework or sit down and be a part of this family."

I suddenly felt really bad for getting him into trouble. I mean, don't get me wrong. Richie was really stupid. And yeah he picked on me, but to see him get slapped by Mama. Ouch . . .

Richie smashed back onto the couch snarling at the TV. He was *pissed*.

Abuela slept through the whole thing.

That night, I crawled into bed and curled up real tight. My head had gone to hurting and I lay down way before everyone else. I heard the clopping of El Jefe's hooves and Pape's wheelchair sqeaking against the floor in the hallway. I got up and waited for their shadows to pass under my doorway. I twisted my doorknob real slow so it wouldn't click. I pulled the door open just enough to stick half my face out.

In the hall, Pape hunched over in his wheelchair holding the Cyclops' swollen red fist in his two hands. Kinda like a baby trying to grasp a basketball. Pape pulled it to his heart and seemed to say "Thank you." Or maybe it was "Please win."

I didn't know 'cause it was in Spanish and he said it so low that I guess it could've been anything. Then Pape started to cry. El Jefe knelt down and held on to Pape real tight. In all my life, I'd never seen my father cry. I didn't really know a man could. After a while, El Jefe stood up kind of the way a cow does after laying down, real sluggish, and pushed Pape to his and Mama's room. It seemed like a forever till El Jefe came back out.

He closed the door and kept his palm on it, his eyes closed like he was praying. What could a dark shadow big as a growling fierce beast pray for and to who? How could he be the Cacooey and hold his palm steady against Pape's door?

He stepped away from the door and clippity-clopped down the hall. Without even looking up, he turned his doorknob and flicked off the hall light. His shadow disappeared in the darkness.

6

All morning, Jo and Mary Alice passed notes back and forth through me about El Jefe. By fourth-period science, Jo's drawings had gone from these stick figures and outlines to almost 3-D. She handed me this one drawing of El Jefe with a bull's head and a muscleman body. Big puffs of smoke came out of his nostrils. He had on these boxing gloves with claws tearing out the knuckles and dripping with blood. And the eyes, he only had one and it was one of the scariest things even I had ever seen Jo draw. When Mary Alice saw it, she got scared like it was going to rip through the lines on the paper. Like he would explode on top of her desk and pick her up by that new lacy button-up shirt and fling her against the wall.

Ross the Floss leaned over Mary Alice's shoulder and saw the drawing. I shifted my eyes to him, so she'd stick it under her folder. He sunk back in his seat and stared out the window. I couldn't figure that gringo.

During lunch, I sat in Tan Land and watched Richie a couple tables away tell the Dark Skins about El Jefe. He moved his body all stiff like in that Frankenstein movie they played at Halloween every year. He moaned and grunted and all the boys went to laughing. Then Richie took some fighter pose and started flailing his arms around all wild and fast. Neither one of us had seen El Jefe train. We could only imagine that his enormous arms moved like machine guns, with the power of bazookas we saw on TV. The guys nodded and grinned all cool and tough. Those flunkies, what a bunch of little boys thinking they were all bad with their stiff baggy jeans and their stupid home tattoos. Most of them should've already been in tenth grade.

"Is your brother really tough?" asked Mary Alice.

"No. He's a pendejo," I said, picking the meat out of my spagetti.

Mary Alice got this goofy look in her eyes watching him.

"Gross," I said to her.

"What?" Mary Alice asked. "You can't talk, Chula. Everyone knows Ross the Floss is crushing on you."

"Shut up," I said, hoping Jo wasn't listening, and she wasn't.

She was too busy to notice. She glared over at Carla's table. Jo hated Carla long before she knocked her out for throwing that volleyball at me. Carla treated us all like dirty Mexicans from the start. Especially ones like me and Jo and Mary Alice who got to do accelerated classes with her or any of her friends. Seemed like there was always someone like Carla to remind you what part of town you lived in and how really round and brown it is 'cept for the sprinkles of pepper and salt.

Once Carla tried to show Jo up in life skills class. Carla realized Jo couldn't make out the words right when she had to read out loud and laughed real big at Jo. It would've been one thing to just have Carla laughing but the whole class joined in and the kids started making fun a lot. That was when Jo went really hard about Squares and especially Carla.

"Check this out," Jo said.

I looked over my shoulder and Ross the Floss was coming over. Oh no. . . .

I turned back around in my seat.

"Chula?" he asked.

"What?" I said, not looking at him.

Even Richie stopped showing off to see what was going on.

"I wanted to ask you something," he said, his voice all soft but serious.

Then it happened just like this.

"What are you doing over here?" Carla snapped at Ross the Floss.

She was right behind me and her voice shredded the insides of my ears. I hunched down a little lower.

"Nothing," he said. "I just wanted to talk to Chula."

"Listen little brother, we don't come to this side," she said.

Jo was fuming.

Carla slammed her hand on the table and got in my face. "Stay away from my brother."

"I wasn't doing him anything," I said, keeping my head down.

She straightened her wicked-witch back with Mitzy right beside her.

"I don't want him to catch your . . ." and then she did it.

She started shaking and rolling her eyes in the back of her head like she was Flashing only she wasn't. And a bunch of kids stared and I wanted to cry. Jo saw the tears bubbling up and didn't so much as blink when she snapped outta her seat. She pounced right on that gringa. A couple of Squares started pulling on Jo and everyone closed in in this circle chanting, "Fight! Fight! Fight!"

I stood up on my seat so I could see and those Squares were holding Jo so she couldn't get loose and Carla was taunting her like some damn locked-up animal. I went to shaking 'cause I was so scared and mad all at the same time. I looked at Ross the Floss who was trying to break through but that gringo wasn't getting nowhere.

I dug through arms and legs and cut all the way in and yanked Carla's hair back. She squealed and hollered like a pig and when she turned around I knew I was in some kind of trouble. She had a good four inches on me and arms as long as telephone poles or close enough 'cause she cracked me so fast and hard the first time I didn't even feel it the second.

I fell to the floor crying 'cause it really hurt. She crawled on top of me and slapped my face and I heard them still saying, "Fight! Fight! Fight!" only it sounded a lot different inside the circle with that gringa on top of me. Kinda like she got bigger and stronger each time they said it.

I wiggled and wiggled but somehow that twig had me pinned. So I just crossed my arms over my face and felt her fists beat into my bones. I thought she might break every one of them until Jo kicked that gringa off me. She grabbed Carla good just when the teachers cut in. All the kids scattered.

That wasn't how it was supposed to be at all. Not one bit. Richie was supposed to stick up for me, that macho pendejo. Only he saw me laying there and just shook his head all disappointed and walked away. Mary Alice was still perched in her seat all big-eyed and bewildered as one of the eighth grade football coaches lifted me up by my arm. I never picked a fight in my whole life and only wanted to fight in one when I was four. Only then, I tell Pape and he tell me what he always tell me, "There's always a better way to solve things."

So when almost every day some kid made fun of me for being so ugly or having Flashes, I kept walking to class trying to concentrate and trying not to think about all the broken glass I remembered in dreams that smelt like hot burning rain.

The principal was out so we got lucky. All of us got a warning 'cept Jo 'cause she admitted that she came busting out of her seat. There's not a whole lot to argue for self-defense when you stick up for someone else's defense I guess. She got a day of In School Suspension starting like right then. When she stood up to leave the office, Jo said to me not to worry about it. "Just hold your head up. Be proud of yourself, Mexican."

But Jo didn't have to go home and face my father all disappointed in me. She didn't have to face nobody 'cept her mom and she didn't really care what Jo did. The vice principal scooped her up by her elbow and led her out. I was left there on the bench with Carla. Her hair just as stuck up in places as she was. She was gonna have a purple eye for sure from where Jo hit her. She turned her head to me and narrowed her eyes.

"What?" she asked, like she was gonna spit fire.

I dropped my eyes to my sneakers.

The secretary gave us passes to go back to class. When we got out into the hall, Carla shoved me and I squeezed my hand into a fist just in case. Even though I didn't really know what to do with a squeezed fist 'cept run.

"Stay away from my little brother. Com—pren—day?"

I wanted to hit her. Hit her so hard she'd never look at me like that again. But I was already in enough trouble. And it wasn't like I could really do her anything anyway.

I watched her cut off down the hall.

I hated being picked on and being all weak-backed to do something about it. I hated that I was scared of almost everything that could come near my head. Mostly, I hated one pink and a blue three times a day so I wouldn't Flash. Why did Pape and me live? I didn't know. What was the point when you gotta be afraid of everything?

Like he kept telling Mama not to let me walk to school alone and he bugged her so much that she started believing something else bad was gonna happen. What could be worse than being all weak-backed and soft-brained?

7

I leaned on the back door, closing it real careful. The house was quiet. Not even the sound of Abuela singing. I went to the cabinet and pulled out the Doritos. All the way home, I thought how I would hide my face. I would fake being sick or pretend to be sleeping and that would keep Pape from seeing my sore lip and pregnant eye. I hadn't seen my eye yet but it had to be bad 'cause it felt even worse than when I got pinkeye in second grade.

I heard a noise. Somebody was there. I

stopped chewing. The basement door was cracked open. The light was on. What if Mama was in the basement doing laundry? What if worse . . . El Jefe?

I grabbed a handful of Doritos and ran through the kitchen. Soon as I come around the corner to the hall, I bounced off El Jefe. I woulda screamed if I hadn't fell right back on my butt.

He leaned down like it took real time and effort to move in any one direction and I started scooting back on my butt, crushing the Doritos in my hand. He stopped moving toward me. I waited.

"What happened?" he asked.

The Cyclops could speak. His voice hung out in the air in these thick soft sounds. Sort of crackling like dead leaves in parts. But it wasn't scary and clawing the way I had imagined. It sounded like . . . a man.

"I fell," I said.

"Not now. Before. When someone hit you."

What did he mean what happened? My lip was swelled and my eye had to look bad and I couldn't believe the bones in my arms weren't sticking out broken the way they were hurting. I thought about being really smart like I would've with Richie but remembered El Jefe was nothing like Richie. In one move, he could finish me quick. Then pack my bags and make it look like I'd run away. They'd all believe it and probably be grateful. Richie for sure anyway.

He reached to touch my face and I winced. He pulled back like a scared boy. How could I scare the Cyclops?

"What happened?" he asked again.

"Just school. Some girl started something with me about—"

I started to tell something about the Flashes when I noticed his head was cocked to the side like a dog's. Like something that was like, listening.

"She just had it coming in a big way," I said.

"I've never fought anyone who had it coming. That must be very different."

"Where's Mama?" I asked.

"She took your father to the doctor."

"Abuela?"

"Sleeping," he said.

At least I wasn't all alone. Not that Abuela asleep or awake really did me much good against something like El Jefe.

He stretched out his club-hand again. I

watched real close as his cracked fingers unfolded into an open palm. A palm with so many lines that you could read ten men's lives in it. El Jefe was big enough to of eaten that many and have room for one more Mexican girl.

"She must have been big," he said.

"Not really."

"Come on," he said. "I know what to do for you."

His hand waited as he slowly lifted back up; his knees cracked like Pop Rocks. The Dark One, the Shape, the Shadow that shrieked at our front door when the light came on kept his leathery hand full of other men's pain open for me to take. I imagined touching it and feeling the blood and death of all those men jolt into me like electricity. What if he'd never held a girl's hand and crushed every bone at the slightest grip?

"Te ayudaré," he said.

"I don't know what you're saying," I said frustrated.

He motioned to take his hand. I got up on my own with moist Dorito crumbs in my hand. I followed him into the kitchen making sure I was far enough back in case he was anything like that drawing Jo did in English.

"Sit down," he said, nodding to the kitchen table. "Please."

I sat, not taking my eyes off him.

He wrapped ice in a bandana that'd been in his pocket Jesus only knows how long. He gave me the bandana and I pressed it to my eye and my eyeball went numb and I wondered if it would roll out and fall to the floor and break like glass. I hated glass.

"You know fighting isn't the smartest thing," he said.

That seemed crazy coming from him. I acted like I couldn't care what he thought. Besides, what did he know about junior high? Richie said he stopped school in second grade. I bet he didn't even know what algebra was. He definitely didn't know what it was like to have gringas make fun of him for being pudgy and shaky and too brown or not brown enough. No one would make fun of the most famous prizefighter in all of Mexico. What did he know, anyway?

"Where does your mother keep the medicine basket?"

I nodded toward the fridge. El Jefe extended his cranelike arms and swept the basket off the top.

He pulled out a chair in front of me. When he reached for my hand holding the ice, I jerked back.

"Put it on your lip," said El Jefe.

He took a cotton ball out of a plastic bag.

"At least you didn't lose any teeth," he said. "Teeth are expensive."

He tapped a cotton ball with alcohol and patted it on my eye.

"Ouch," I said, squinting and squirming and doing everything but getting up.

"It's only a scratch," he said.

"It still hurts."

"Sorry," he said, fishing around in the medicine basket.

His eye patch seemed more cool than it had at breakfast that morning. Softer.

"Is that from the dogs?" I asked. "The scar on your eye."

He dipped a Q-tip in the Monkey's Blood. "Raise your head," he said.

"Richie says that's from real South African monkeys," I said. "When he was little, he was always getting into fights so Mama would have to put Monkey's Blood on him. That way he could climb and run faster than anyone else."

El Jefe reached for a Band-Aid.

"I almost never got any Monkey Blood," I said to him. "Maybe that's why I can't fight."

"I wish I didn't fight," he said. "I wish I could do something smart. Like go to school like you." He pressed the Band-Aid on and I squealed. "But that's not what was in the plan for me." He smiled a little but not for real. "Plans are hard."

"Pape says you can be anything you want in this world. Richie says that's true if you're not a girl."

"Listen to your Pape. He's a smart man."

El Jefe poured two aspirin on the table and put the medicine basket back on top of the fridge.

"Look where it got him. A good job with a bunch of gringos giving him nothing but trouble so he'd drink all the time," I said. "He'll never walk again you know. His back busted in three places. He just flew."

"He's still walking," said El Jefe. "Not upright but in his heart." He handed me a cup of water. "Your lip's gonna hurt for a while. No salsa. Your eye will be better tomorrow."

I swallowed the aspirin. "Are you going to win tomorrow night?" I asked him.

He smiled and asked, "Do you want some ice cream?"

el Jefe pointed to the ice cream he wanted, holding up his fingers for two scoops.

"Don'tcha want sprinkles?" I asked him. "They're free here."

For a corner market, they had all kinds of sprinkles. El Jefe bent down and considered them real careful. There were chocolate ones; red, whites, and blues; green and orange ones; neon pink ones with blue dots. But the yellows. He liked those the most.

He nodded to the macho-macho guy behind the counter who hadn't taken his eyes off El Jefe for one second. He handed the ice cream to El Jefe like he was afraid to get too close, to even touch his fingers. El Jefe gave me three dollars and left.

I put the money on the counter but that macho-macho guy was stretching his skinny neck around the scratch-off bin to catch another look at El Jefe.

"Who is that?" he asked me.

El Jefe stood outside the glass door. His one eye wedged between phone card flyers watching me.

"The Cacooey," I said taking my change.

Walking down the street, El Jefe seemed more like a giant child licking his big double heaps of vanilla ice cream. Sprinkles scattered like lost children hoping to find their mothers soon. I sipped on a can of Pepsi 'cause Mama never gave us Cokes 'cause she said they make you get all swollen up inside. Maybe I'd pop before dinner and not have to face Pape or Richie or even Abuela singing to the sky.

We crossed the street, passing a couple of boys from the elementary all big-eying us on their low-rider bikes. They stared like they'd never seen nothing like El Jefe and I guess they hadn't.

"Where are all the children?" asked El Jefe, following me inside the gates to the Playground.

"It useta be real pretty here," I said to him, looking at the broken seesaw. "But the gangs started slingin' down here for a while. They still do, I guess."

We walked around. His eyes followed the chain fence full of Styrofoam cups.

"Abulea says it smells like sadness here now. Like tears that nobody wiped away after crying real hard."

He watched a plastic bag flap in the top of a tree.

"Why don't you speak Spanish?" he asked.

"I just never really got it. It sounds like noise in my ears. Kind of like gargling with mouthwash. But it sucks 'cause it feels like sometimes I'm the only Mexican who can't speak it. My friends go to talking in Spanish, my only two friends, and I nod and later they'll say something about what they said earlier and I'm like, 'Uh, I wasn't listening.' I guess they know though."

He smiled at me. It was funny how he listened like he cared. No one ever had time or if they did, they just didn't get what I was saying.

"Spanish is easy," said El Jefe. "You just listen with your heart and the words move like flavors, colors. Like, agua dulce."

"Dulce is sweet. I know that," I said.

"Don't think. The brain gets in the way in Spanish. It knows too much."

I watched these ponytail tough girls from junior high come strutting up and kick up real high on the swings. I wondered if their mamas liked them being so tough.

"Why do you take those pills? Are you sick?" he asked.

"I got hit in the head too hard in the car accident and my brain got all big. I had this . . ."

I started to say it like all official only I'd never had to say it all official 'cept to the doctor, who made me repeat it back to him to make sure I understood. And I was like, "I ain't no retard." And sometimes I think, man, school makes some people so stupid 'cause that doctor had me repeat like everything. But anyways, when I did say it out loud to the doctor, Mama was sitting there and she just dropped her head like it was heavier than two weeks of laundry and Richie's bad grades. She breathed all deep and held her rosary in her pocket. She never carried it until the accident.

El Jefe still looked at me like I was going to finish so it seeped out of my mouth like a really bad
taste, like black-licorice bubble gum.

"Seizure. You know what that is?" I asked him.

He paused. "It's where you shake hard," he
said. "I seen a boxer do it."

" 'Cause you hit him so hard?"

"No, he had . . ." El Jefe's mouth started the
word, hesitated, then, ". . . epilepsy. Is that what
they call it in English?"

I couldn't believe the Cyclops knew what *It*
was called. He didn't pass second. How could he
not say something stupid like "You got the devil in
you" or "You've been touched" or "You have
AIDS" or "You're on drugs" or all the things people in the Circle said to me or Mama or behind
our backs especially at church. And they said it so
much that we didn't even go no more. How could
he of all people know the official word?

"Yeah, that's what the doctors call it, only
don't say that in the house. The word makes
Mama sick to her belly. We just don't talk about it,
okay?"

He nodded.

I didn't even talk about it with Jo and Mary
Alice 'cause it made them all nervous and I

thought they might stop hanging out with me like everybody else did. Still there was something in the way he looked at me made me feel like it was okay.

"You only have two friends? Why?" he asked.

"For real? Parents don't let their kids hang out with me anymore."

His forehead wrinkled all up like he was trying real hard to get it. "But why?" he asked again.

" 'Cause . . . almost everybody in the Circle says I'm possessed by the devil or I'm a witch or some crazy thing like that. When I went back to school after the accident, I was in sixth then, *all* the kids stared at me to see if I'd go to shaking." He listened so closely. "And it happened a lot. Mostly in the mornings, mostly till they got the pills right. But one time, I shook so hard they had to call the ambulance to the school. They took me to the emergency room and everything. Mama just kept praying and praying and you know what, I don't even know if she really does anymore. She says she does but . . ." And I dropped my head. "So I guess I just got two friends 'cause nobody wants to be around anybody who pees their pants even if they don't mean to."

Then all at once everything was quiet and I

was nervous like crazy 'cause I never said any of that out loud. And El Jefe didn't say nothing. He just stood there with his ice cream dripping down the cone and onto his meat hook hand. He was thinking so hard that I thought he might fall right down and shake too when—

"People are strange," said El Jefe.

"People suck."

"Did it scare you? When you shook?" asked El Jefe.

"I can't remember. It's like, there's a before. Then there's an after. But no middle. And I was real tired like I'd been running for days and days. It really embarrassed everybody, you know?"

"No."

"Well, I'm scary," I said to him.

I started to think I made him mad 'cause he got to looking at me real hard. I held the can of Pepsi close to my chest in case I had to fling it at him to get away. Then this crooked grin edged onto his face.

"You're twelve," he said. "And your name is Chula, Beautiful. The only thing scary about you is if you believe what people say. And they will say lots of things, most of them not true."

I'd never talked about the Flashes before and

never thought I'd be telling the Cyclops. There was something so gentle about him that made it so hard to believe he'd killed men for not much more than a cup of coffee. I wanted to ask him a dozen questions. What was it like to win? How did he get so strong? Where was his mother? Did she miss him? What was Pape like back when he was younger?

But before I could ask him anything Richie came strutting along the fence behind Freddy and a couple of new Dark Skins. They all had their hair full of gel and their dead-cat stiff baggy jeans peeked outta their sloppy too-big T-shirts. One of the Dark Skins grinned at the girls on the swings when he came inside the gate. Both girls grinned back and all I kept thinking was seeds. Lots and lots of seeds.

"Wow, check the marks," said Freddy, grinning at my fat eye. "Richie, you didn't tell me your little sister was down like this. What's the other girl look like?"

Freddy held out his hand to El Jefe. He didn't take it.

"Are you kidding?" said Richie. "Mike Tyson here didn't even get one punch in."

"Shut up, pendejo," I said to Richie.

"Ooooo," said the Dark Skins.

Richie asked all slow like I was some kinda retard, "¿Por qué no me callas?" He looked to Freddy. "My own sister can't speak Spanish. You believe that?"

"It's okay. She's still Mexican," Freddy said, putting his hand on my shoulder like we'd been best friends forever and ten years. "And that's power."

El Jefe's hand clamped onto Freddy's arm twisting it back behind him so fast you could almost not see it happen. How could something so big move that fast?

"El Jefe," said Richie. "He didn't mean nothing."

The veins in Freddy's face flared. His arm twisted so far back that only luck kept it from snapping. Snapping just like one of them wishbones out of a Thanksgiving turkey.

El Jefe snarled, then let him go.

Freddy popped back up all cocky but rubbing his arm like crazy. No way did that not hurt. The Dark Skins pulled Freddy by the shoulders. He shirked them off as he backed out toward the Playground gate.

El Jefe latched onto Richie's arm. "¿Por qué?"

asked El Jefe, nodding toward Freddy and the Dark Skins.

"Mi familia."

El Jefe spoke real fast in Spanish with me only catching *family* again and him looking at me somewhere in the middle. Richie kept his eyes on the ground like he wasn't hearing none of it.

"Richie, now," shouted Freddy at the Playground gates.

Richie looked at Freddy but El Jefe's grip tightened and must've burned from the way Richie's face got all scrunched up.

"El Jefe," I said, but he didn't look away.

It was like I wasn't even standing there the way he looked at Richie. And Richie, that pendejo, he met El Jefe eye to eye with that dumbhead cockiness he used on Pape.

"¿Por qué?" asked El Jefe again but with a darkness across his face.

"El Jefe, por favor," said Richie, snarling with every word.

Then he spoke all fast so I didn't have no chance of understanding till Richie's eyes shifted to the Dark Skins. He didn't want El Jefe to make trouble.

I thought El Jefe might rip Richie's arm off the way he was looking at him. But then his grip loosened and Richie flung away to keep face with the Dark Skins and especially with rat-nosed Freddy. He jogged off to catch up to them.

"Why did you get all mad at him?" I asked.

El Jefe shook his head and threw his ice cream in the rusty garbage can.

"I don't know."

"Richie just likes to act all tough. He won't do nobody nothing. Besides, Freddy's just a show-off really."

"No," said El Jefe, watching Freddy disappear around the corner. "I know boys like him. There's too much darkness in their hearts." His eyes were so serious. "Stay safe from him, Chula. You understand?"

I shrugged. "I guess."

It was dark when we started back. It seemed like we'd been gone from the house for days 'cause we got to talking about school and Carla, about Mexico and how Pape useta outsmart anybody who wanted to fight him growing up. El Jefe even taught me some simple Spanish and it actually didn't sound so weird in my head for once. If he stayed long enough, I could speak it almost as good as my friends in no time. Why I wanted El Jefe to stay then when the morning before I just hoped he wouldn't swallow me with breakfast, I didn't know. Maybe it was 'cause we seemed a lot alike. Only people really respected him.

When we hit the edge of my neighborhood, whispers went from porch to stoop to front yard. Everybody watched us walk past. Their eyes moved up his towering dark face that only had human shape when he stepped in patches of yellow from a streetlight. His body seemed heavier and thicker and made of bricks and boulders at night. With the sun tucked in and Night on its watch, it made El Jefe look like the thing Abuela had described before he came: Death.

But still it was the first time since the accident that when I walked by I didn't feel like I had to drop my head 'cause they were all talking about how messed up I was. Right then, I was with the most loved man in Mexico City, in all of Mexico. No one could hurt me.

"They're talking about you, El Jefe," I said. "That must feel good."

He said nothing.

"El Jefe?" I asked.

His head tilted a little toward me. Enough to let me know he heard but said nothing. Had the darkness changed him? Thickened his blood and sharpened his teeth into switchblades? Had that rabid poison boiled in his veins and changed him from a man into a beast that if he spoke, only the words of Death would crawl outta his mouth like scorpions ready to sting?

"Don't be afraid of what other people see, Chula." His voice was deeper and sounded like it had traveled through the roots of a dead tree. "Their eyes are not your eyes. Sus ojos no son tus ojos. ¿Bueno?"

As we turned the corner toward home, a couple of little kids came chasing each other. One of them, this Slinky of a boy, crashed right into El Jefe and landed just like I had that afternoon. Right on his butt. Only when El Jefe reached to help the boy he *screamed* "Cacooey! Cacooey!" And ran with his friends.

I looked at El Jefe and saw that it hurt his feelings. I don't know why but I took his hand. We said nothing as we walked the last four blocks to the house.

When we got home, Mama had fallen asleep in the living room. Pape slumped in his wheelchair. El Jefe pushed Pape's chair down the hall. I followed behind him and watched from the bedroom door as he lifted Pape out of the chair and carried him like a sleepy son to the bed. Pape looked so small and delicate in El Jefe's steel and rock arms. He slid Pape's slippers off. Then he got on his knees beside the bed like a little kid with his hands pressed together in an *A*. He bowed his head and then he seemed so much smaller than I could've ever imagined.

I wanted to know so bad what the servant of the devil could ask God for. Would God even listen? He hadn't to me when I went through the glass and saw Mama crushed more than my bones at the hospital, and when that doctor said to me "Do you understand?" and I'm like "I ain't no retard" and I ain't. God didn't listen when Richie started running harder and faster, fighting more and soaking himself in Monkey's Blood so he could outclimb and outrun anybody. Only it just made Richie run from the family faster than anything else and that seemed stupid. Not that I was calling God stupid.

El Jefe knelt there for what felt like days 'cause of how he stayed real still and focused. I could almost see streams of light coming from the tips of his dry fingers. I swear on the Virgin that some kind of warmth came from his fingers pointing up, even if it was only the spill of the streetlight from outside. I know I saw something I'd never seen before.

That night, nothing could get me settled in bed. I imagined the roof blowing off and plaster scattering like snow all over the Circle. Children coming out in their pajamas singing "Cielito Lindo" and dancing, playing hopscotch with real chalk and not the butts of rocks. Their parents smiling and sipping cans of Pepsi or sweet, sweet iced tea.

I imagined the stars that never seemed to fall in our Texas galloping like wild mustangs straight for us and just before crashing and exploding into us they'd vanish like them fireworks Richie buys every Fourth of July even if it's illegal.

That night, I decided I wanted to be as strong as El Jefe. I wanted the world to love me and think I was larger than the word *large* could ever be.

I was staring down at my morning pills when my stupid brother went to pounding on the bathroom door.

"Ay dios mio, Chula. I'm gonna explode out here," said Richie.

"I'm almost done," I said. "In about an hour."

"Mama!" he yelled.

I slipped the pills in my jeans' front pocket and snapped open the door.

"Shut up already."

"Nice shiner," he said, squeezing my cheeks.

I slapped his hand away.

"You'll never get a man," said Richie.

"Like I want one so I can listen to him whine like you. 'Mama, she won't get outta the bathroom.' You wouldn't be calling her so fast if she knew you were still hangin' with the Skins."

He banged my shoulder as he walked in the bathroom and shoved me from out of the doorway.

"Don't see you running to tell her you were out with El Jefe yesterday."

"You're just scared I might get poison in my veins and swell up so big I could beat your head in."

"Pues, the only thing you're getting is fatter." And he slammed the door.

The first thing I wanted to do when I got strong was get him back. That was for sure.

I sat at the breakfast table and El Jefe was nearly done with his trough of food. Mama was so busy cooking in the kitchen she didn't really notice that I had my hair down to cover my three-colored eye and split lip. El Jefe motioned for me to pull my hair a little to the left.

"I'm cooking for Tío Tony," said Mama. "He's

taking a bunch of food to the guys at work who've been telling everyone about the fight. So you'll have to eat cereal."

She didn't even raise her head from the stove.

I poured out a bowl of cereal and looked at El Jefe, who half-grinned at me. We were like fighters who sat down after a really hard night to talk about how we won our matches only I lost. Still, he made me feel like I didn't.

Richie came bouncing in wearing a polo with his hair slick and flat. Mama saw him and stepped back.

"Okay, what judge do you gotta see today?" she asked.

He kicked into his polished white Nikes.

"Pues . . . it's school pictures." Then he cocked his head my direction with the grin of two devils and three wives.

Holy oh holy big-time trouble. School pictures and me with an eye that looked like a thunderstorm at red sunset. Mama glanced at me, only noticing my one-size-too-small T-shirt of Selena and said, "No mam. Go put on the yellow shirt your Tía Irma buy you in May."

The yellow shirt didn't fit in May and it sure

wasn't gonna fit now. Not to mention it had these really lacy frills around the collar that always made my neck itch like crazy loco crazy.

"I mean it Chula," said Mama, pulling a tray outta the oven. "We're not putting a school picture in that living room with Selena on your chest. God rest her soul nonetheless. Andale!"

Richie had a mouth full of teeth all grinning at me. He was dying to tell her about my face. My brother hadn't forgotten the night before last when I got him slapped. Right then he couldn't wait for his *accelerated* sister to get half her butt chewed off.

I put my hands on the table and eased up careful not to move my head too quickly. I pushed the chair in all quiet.

"Hey Mama," said Richie.

That was it. Grounded for forty years. I never been in a fight. Never started one but it didn't matter. I was barely twelve, almost thirteen in like eight months, but so what 'cause I hadn't started my period, grew breasts or lived somewhere else. Which meant I could get grounded and maybe even worse, spanked in front of Richie.

Richie held his taunting grin.

"Can I have cheese in my taquitos?" he asked.

¿Queso? That was it? Pendejo.

"Do you see taquitos for you? Cereal this morning," she said.

I marched out of the kitchen and turned the corner to the hall when Pape wheeled up and saw my face. I should've stayed in the kitchen.

"Where is your mother?" he asked.

"Pape," I said.

"ANSWER ME!" he said, in a voice I'd heard only for Richie.

"In the kitchen," I said, not looking at him.

"Elena," Pape said.

Mama came around the corner.

"¿Qué pasó, Hector?"

"Chula has something to show you." He pointed for me to turn around and I did and she—

"What, you're starting fights now?" asked Mama.

"Busted . . . ," Richie said, coming out of the kitchen slurping a spoonful of cereal.

"Shut your mouth," I said to him as El Jefe came to the doorway.

"Hello, I'm talking to you Chula," said Mama.

"No, I'm not starting fights. . . . This girl at school—"

"No mam. We do not handle our problems with violence," said Mama. "It is a gift that they let you attend that program at that school. You're still too young to understand, but you listen to me. You think it was bad them calling here and saying you're a retard? Well a hoodlum is worse 'cause that's something you can control."

She said it. She said *retard* out loud in front of Pape, El Jefe, Abuela sitting in the corner of the living room daydreaming and worst of all and no way could it be any worse in front of my stupid-mean wish-I-were-dead brother, Richie. He looked liked he'd hit the Texas jackpot and he had.

"I ain't no retard," I said.

"Retard, retard. My sister's a retard," sang Richie.

"Callate," said Mama and he hushed up but grinned ear-to-big-fat-ear.

She snapped her head back at me and said, "You will go in that bathroom and take your pills—"

"I already take them—"

"Do not get smart with me right now. You will take your pills and get my makeup and play grown-up. You will ask them to take your pictures with the retakes in a month or whenever they give them and you will come straight home after school just with your brother."

"Ay . . . ," moaned Richie.

She swung her head back at him and he quickly shrugged and went back in the kitchen.

"We do not fight in this family," she said. "Do you understand?"

I bit down real hard on every word that wanted to come slithering like ten ten-headed snakes outta my mouth. Angry cottonmouths loaded with dripping venom.

I looked at El Jefe standing in the kitchen doorway with his paws swallowing the doorframe. He was a fighter and they weren't yelling at him. They weren't telling him nothing. And then I started thinking, they *weren't* telling him nothing.

I glared at Pape and said, " 'Cause there's always a better way. Right?"

And right then he saw I knew. I knew he hadn't found a better way.

"Chula, go do as I told you," said Mama, only I kept looking at Pape.

He dropped his head and pushed his wheelchair past me.

"NOW, Chula," she said.

Mama apologized to El Jefe as I walked down the hall. He didn't say anything. I guess when you're strong you don't have to.

On the way to school, I followed several steps behind Richie and his stupid friends. All the way through the Circle, it seemed like people looked out their windows or stood on their porches just to see us. Even the ones that had somewhere to go work, and that seemed less and less, they looked too. It was the weirdest thing. Could missing one dose of my medicine make me strong already? Could they see I wasn't needing nothing to keep me from falling down?

But the last thing I expected walking past Tía Josie's house that morning was Tía Josie waiting for me.

"Chula," she said, walking up to me with her face made up all pretty.

Richie stopped.

"Hey, Richie," she said.

He nodded but didn't leave his friends.

"How are you?" she asked, her voice as soft as velvet.

"Okay, I guess."

She smiled, and not like when people do it to

be all polite. She meant it. "You've really grown up. Your hair. It's beautiful."

If it wasn't for the noisy city bus blowing by, I don't know what I would've done 'cause it was all weird how she was staring at me. Like I was somebody else. Somebody she knew a whole lot better than me.

"I came to see you at the hospital," she said.

"No one said nothing to me."

"Yeah, well, your mother wasn't exactly thrilled, you know."

I nodded. Mama probably had to pray extra just to get the thought of Tía Josie outta her head.

"Look, I know Elena doesn't want you talking to me but I'm worried about you, Chula."

"Huh?"

"This man, the prizefighter from Mexico. Everyone's talking about him. Saying you were alone with him yesterday. It isn't safe for you to be with him. Your mother knows that."

"No, no. He's really okay. Yesterday I come home from school, right, and he fixed my eye. Look, it ain't even big no more and he bought me ice cream and he told me all kinds of things about Mexico. He's not what people think, Tía."

She leaned in and put her hands on my arms.

Her face so soft and warm. How could Mama not want to look at a face so warm?

"Tell your mother the offer still stands," she said.

I shook my head. "What do you mean?"

"Just tell her, Chula." The back of her hand gently brushed the length of my scar. "Take care."

She walked back to her tiny house.

"Come on, Chula," said Richie already walking with the dumb-head twins.

Soon as I caught up with them, Richie dropped back asking, "What was that all about?"

"Nothing."

"If Mama knew you were talking to her, she wouldn't think it was nothing."

"If Mama knew you had a cell phone 'cause you were running with Freddy, you'd be on the street tomorrow."

"Right, she's gonna kick out the ONLY person in our house that ISN'T messed up."

He laughed and stepped up in the middle of Raul and Paul.

I was almost to my locker when Jo yanked me from behind and pulled me into the restroom. I dropped my books all over.

"What?" I asked all freaked out.

"Everybody's talking and you don't call us, your best friends?" asked Jo.

Mary Alice leaned against the sink.

"Call you about what?" I said. "I just come to school–"

"Mexican, you were out with him last night," said Jo.

"So . . . ?"

Jo's mouth dropped like I made some huge mistake like when I got her new Diamondback lowrider banana seat run over by the garbage truck.

Mary Alice swallowed softly and said, "He killed a little boy in Mexico."

My mouth dropped. "What?" I asked.

"It's true. The kid was like ten and he killed him," said Jo.

"Right," I said.

"I'm not playing you, Chula," said Jo.

"Okay, how do you know?" I asked.

"What?" Jo said, shocked.

"Pues, you're the news flash. How do you know?"

Jo looked at Mary Alice.

"Your mom told my mom before he even came," said Mary Alice. "And she told me this morning, so I'd stay away from your house."

I shook my head. "No way," I said. "She would've told me. She wouldn't let him in the house if he did something like that."

I started picking up my books.

"Thanks, Jo. My algebra folder's soaked." I stood up, wiping my folder off on my jeans. "Can we go now?" I asked them.

"Chula, even you said you never seen nothing like him, right?" asked Jo.

"Yeah," I said.

"That even your abuela said he was dark as Death," Jo said.

The warning bell for first period rang.

I shook my head and went to the door. "Stop it already. You're not gonna scare me," I said. "Look, believe what you want. But he's not like people say. I don't know how to tell you different."

"Whatever," said Jo, heading out the door.

Mary Alice followed her.

All morning, all I could think about was what Jo said. It didn't make no sense. How could he kill a boy and be like he was to me?

At lunch, I put up my tray and went over to Richie's table. The guys looked at me like I was some kinda zombie.

"What do you want?" Richie said annoyed.

"I gotta talk to you," I said.

"Talk to me later," he said keeping face with the grinning dumb-heads.

I leaned down. "Talk to me now or I'll tell them how you messed around with that ugly girl over the summer."

He shoved me away and thought about what I said. Then he got up.

"What?" said Richie.

"Jo said something to me earlier. About El Jefe."

"This is why you're bugging me? 'Cause of girlie talk?"

"Ay, I just wanna know if it's true," I said. "Did Mama tell you El Jefe killed a boy?"

"Hey, Richie," said Raul. "We're going out back to . . ." And he squeezed his fingers like he was puffing on a joint.

"I gotta go," said Richie to me.

I grabbed his arm. "Richie, come on, don't be all stupid, just tell me."

"Pues, he kill a lot of people, Chula. I don't know. I gotta go."

He cut between the tables and went out the double doors.

For some reason it felt like he was going a lot farther than out behind school.

No way did El Jefe kill a boy. How could I go believing something like that?

10

the door to the basement was cracked and the smaCK-THUD Bam-BAM slapped up the wooden stairs. I had my head resting on my hands and could hear his breathing, his panting . . . the roar.

Mama came up the stairs and dropped a basket of laundry on the table.

"Why aren't you doing your homework?" she asked.

"I don't feel like it."

"Oh, that's a real special life you're living.

Maybe I should not feel like cooking dinner or washing your shirts."

"I heard something at school today," I said. "About El Jefe."

Mama snapped one of my shirts and spread it on the table to fold.

"They say he killed a boy in Mexico." I waited for her to say "You're crazy, Chula. You're outta your mind."

She kept folding.

"It's not true, right?" I asked.

"What do you want me to tell you, Chula?" asked Mama.

"Tell me the truth. Tell me he didn't do him nothing."

"Where's your brother?" asked Mama.

"Pues, I don't know," I said, getting up and shoving the chair against the table. "And I don't care."

"Watch it," Mama warned.

"You knew," I said. "You knew and you didn't say nothing."

I stormed down the hall. Shut my door and put my dinky white straw chair under the door-knob with the Virgin as a doorstop. Nobody was stronger than the Virgin 'cept Jesus and he was hanging in the bathroom next to the ad flyers and extra toilet paper.

I pulled down the bleached-out yellow shade and tore open my box of stuffed animals all squished together. Richie had talked me into boxing them the first week of junior high, saying how I was never gonna grow up if I had dollies all over my bed. But right then, I didn't care. I just wanted to forget that Squaretown junior high and the Flashes and me getting heavier because of the one pink and a blue and the weeks of being all depressed and the counselors telling me why and me not listening and the headaches and Mama fighting with Pape about bills and the smell of broken glass in my nose and burnt refried beans and everything I forgot to say to Pape when he come home and everything I can't remember. I hopped in the middle of my bed surrounded by teddy bears, unicorns, blonde-haired dolls, stringy stuffed dogs, and puffy cats and waited for the day to just be over.

But it wasn't long till Richie beat on my door, rocking the Virgin a little side to side but she held her ground.

"Dinner's ready," he said.

"I have a headache, pendejo. Go away."

He waited a while 'cause I could see his shadow under the door before he left. Anyways, I knew dinner was ready. I'd been smelling fajitas since they crawled down the hall and squeezed around the door edges. Man, I was hungry like no tomorrow. Only I wasn't coming outta there. Not to sit at the same table with Mama.

Then Mama went to knocking on my door. "Chula, dinner," she said.

And I said, "I ain't hungry."

And then she knew something was wrong and told me, "Open the door right now." She tried the knob but it wouldn't open. "What are you doing in there?"

"Nothing. I'm sleeping."

Then she pushed on the door and it started to open.

"I'm not kidding. Open this door or you're not going to Mary Alice's party next weekend. You won't leave this house for months."

I got up and moved the Virgin to the side and slid the chair out from under the knob. I opened the door and there was everybody but Abuela.

Mama pushed past me and flicked on the over-head light.

"What were you doing in here?" she asked.

"Nothing. I was sleeping," I said.

After she inspected the room, she turned back to me and stared at me like I had something to say.

"You want to tell me something?" she asked.

"I ain't got nothing to tell," I said. "Do you?"

She was pissed. She looked to Richie then me.

"What were you doing with Tía Josie this morning?" she asked.

I spun around glaring at Richie.

"He was there too," I said. "How else would he know?"

"I don't care if the Pope was there giving a baptismal. You know how much trouble she is?"

"No," I said.

"What?"

"I don't know what trouble she is," I said. "You never let her around. What did she ever do to us?"

"Enough, do you hear me? What are we to do with you, Chula? I feel like I can't trust you."

"But I ain't done nothing. I go to school. I

come home. I didn't walk with my friends. Not that I really have many no more—"

"Don't you raise your voice to me. You think there's some kind of thing that makes you special because you're sick?"

I started biting down hard.

"That you can get away with being like this? Well, no mam. We have all tried our best. This man," she said, pointing to El Jefe, "has come from Mexico to fight so that you can have a roof over your head—"

"Or drop it on me," I said under my breath.

"What?" she asked, and she wasn't kidding.

I just shook my head.

Mama turned back and spoke real fast in Spanish, knowing I wouldn't catch much of it, then shut the door behind her.

"Now you listen here," she said. "Tonight is everything for this family. El Jefe's been out there worried about you. That man doesn't need to worry about anything but getting in that ring and winning. So you want to pull little stunts? You want attention? Well you have mine. ¿Comprende?"

My gums hurt from biting so hard.

She yanked my wrist. "Do you hear me in there?"

Her eyes. I'd never seen them so empty. They were two deep holes with dull gray color along the edges.

"I ain't a retard," I said, punching her in the face with every word.

Mama hit me only three maybe four times in my life and I always deserved it.

But the way she grabbed my wrist, you'd think I was something she meant to shatter into a thousand pieces. She was getting quicker. Not fast, just quicker.

"Good," she said.

Her grip loosened. The blood raced back to my skin around the imprint of her thin fingers. I stood there mad to tears but not making a sound. No way was I gonna make a sound in front of those eyes.

"How could you not tell me?" I asked her. "He killed a boy in Mexico."

"We had no other choices, Chula. We have nothing."

"You're a liar."

"What did you say?"

"Tía said to tell you the offer still stands. That means money, don't it?" I asked.

"Enough. Go wash your face and eat dinner," she said, walking to the door. "We're leaving for the warehouse in half an hour."

Mama opened the door and left.

She knew and let El Jefe in our house and fed him our tamales and rice and huevos con papas and even tortillas made by her hands and her time. She'd let a killer, not just of men who got in the ring all on their stupid own but of a boy, sleep in Richie's room and dream of fire and rage and blood. And she didn't tell me nothing and I went for ice cream with him and listened to his soft talk and he let me think he was somebody else. Somebody good.

She knew and said nothing to me and Tía did. Tía Josie of all people, who should've hated me just as much as Mama hated her. We didn't say her nothing about Esperanza. We didn't even send flowers.

I wiped my face off on my shirt and walked outta the room. El Jefe stood at the end of the hall listening to Mama. Her hand rested on his chest only for a moment. Then she left to the kitchen.

He turned to me. It seemed like we looked at each other forever. Like there was nothing else in the whole house. Nothing but me and him. And he knew that I knew.

11

el Jefe's oak mouthpiece branded with the word *Morte* sat on top of a stack of towels. They had us in a pasty, brown-carpet room that looked like it useta be somebody's office. El Jefe sat on a desk while Tío Tony leaned over speaking Spanish to him. Streams of sweat poured down El Jefe, racing from his chest to his trunks. He kept squeezing his fingers into his taped palms. Never once looking Tío in the eye.

Outside the office, the crowd in the warehouse stomped their feet and roared 'cause there was another fight going on. But through all the noise outside, Tío focused only on El Jefe.

A couple of guys from the Circle Tío Tony had got to work El Jefe's corner came in. Both of them had fought Bobby "Golden Gloves" Dragon and went down in the first minute so it seemed really stupid to have them helping El Jefe. Not that he probably needed a lot of help anyway.

One of them whispered in Tío's ear. Tío straightened up and looked to us. He nodded to Pape. Pape took Mama's hand and she turned and scooted Richie and me out. El Jefe was still squeezing his fingers into his palms when Mama pushed me toward the door.

She walked ahead of me. I stopped. El Jefe stood and when he did he made Tío look like one of them tiny green toy soldiers that come like fifty in a pack. And Tío was no small man.

El Jefe went to a corner, knelt down and—

"NOW, Chula," said Mama.

I turned and went with her.

There were just as many white faces as brown ones filling up the warehouse. Men stood in the doorways and crowded all around the ring. Pape had wheeled up just a few feet from El Jefe's corner with his hands clasped together, probably praying. Mama had been since before we left the house.

Richie, Mama and me went up the bleachers and crunched into the seventh row. I made sure to put Richie between Mama and me. I wanted to be as far from her as I could even if that was just one seat.

Then the crowd howled and cheered and parted as El Jefe made his way to the ring. Even the referee seemed surprised at the size of El Jefe. The referee waved Bobby "Golden Gloves" Dragon and El Jefe to the center of the ring. They stood toe to toe as he told them the rules which we all knew weren't rules really. Golden Gloves smirked at El Jefe like he was a filthy mangy dog he couldn't wait to kick. El Jefe kept his eyes to the mat. The referee finished and both fighters nodded, touching gloves, only Golden Gloves took a shot at El Jefe's chin right after.

The crowd roared and booed and Richie was on his feet shouting all kinds of things when Mama pulled him back to his seat.

El Jefe walked to his corner and for a second I

thought he saw me among the sea of faces. He sat on what seemed like a little kid's stool and bowed his head. Tío Tony whispered in El Jefe's ear and he lightly nodded, his eyes still nowhere but down.

"What if he loses?" I asked Richie.

"He never loses, *retard*," said Richie.

I glared at him and he grinned all big tossing buttery popcorn in his mouth. Chomping real dramatic like he was eating my heart.

Freddy stepped through the crowd on the floor below with the Dark Skins following like some kind of stupid brown sheep.

Richie scooted down in his seat. He didn't want to be seen with me and Mama at the Thursday night fights for nothing.

"Hey, Freddy!" I shouted. "Freddy!"

Richie pulled me into him. Freddy scanned the stands.

"Quit screwing around, Chula," Richie said.

Mama swatted Richie on the back of the head.

"Ay, Mama," said Richie.

"You better not be hanging out with that cabrón," warned Mama.

"I ain't doing nothing," said Richie, pushing me back up in my seat.

Tío stepped out of the ring. El Jefe was finally alone. Alone and sitting on that tiny stool with his head down. I wanted him to win. I wanted him to lose. I wanted us to all go home and have sopapillas with vanilla ice cream and pretend we didn't need him to be the Cyclops with fists of blinding peppers and acid. I wanted it to not be true that he killed a little boy so Richie could get to know him the way I did at the Playground and Pape could get him a good job where nobody had to get hurt. I mean, he COULD lose. Everyone loses sometimes.

The crowd went to chanting, shouting, *"Jefe! Jefe! Jefe! . . ."*

The bell rang.

Golden Gloves sparkled out of his corner, his white satin trunks moved like gentle waves in the Gulf of Mexico. He pranced around the ring firing off his jabs, flinging his hands in the air in victory. El Jefe hadn't even got up off his stool and already that gringo was acting like he beat us.

El Jefe crossed his chest in the name of the holies and kissed his glove. I'll never forget the cocky Squaretown grin on Golden Gloves when he made his way to the center of the ring. Waving El Jefe on with his rich white glove.

El Jefe stood. The stool was swept away. El Jefe took two steps outta his corner, his bloodred gloves like boulders nestled close to his sweaty chest. His shiny crimson trunks were lined with black and gold snakes slithering up the sides and around the waist. His scuffed black boots were burnt deep along the tips and his red coiled laces seemed to cut into him—be him.

Golden Gloves plowed forward and swung for El Jefe's brick jaw. Like a strong tree in a tropical storm, El Jefe leaned slightly, dodging. Golden Gloves's smirk fell right off. He never missed his first punch. NEVER.

The crowd was so loud. Fists pumping in the air.

Then a darkness swept El Jefe's face like when he grabbed Richie at the Playground. But this was darker. I'd never seen nothing like it. It was like watching hot tar fill up where the white of his eye should've been.

El Jefe's right arm wound back. His veins flared and glistened. His jaw constricted as he sank his teeth into that oak mouthpiece. His eye slanted as his head tilted down.

Mama smiled. Pape clapped. Richie shouted, "Kill 'im! Kill 'im Diablo!"

And El Jefe swung. CRASH! Golden Gloves's mouthpiece shot out with a trail of spit.

Richie flew outta his seat cheering. Pumping his fist like crazy.

Golden Gloves's legs wobbled. He pinched the mouthpiece off the mat. Scrambling to get away from El Jefe. From that eye.

Golden Gloves swung. His glove slid off El Jefe's chest. Then El Jefe pounded on him.

CRASH! CRASH-CRASH . . .

Golden Gloves bounced on the ropes—

CRASH!

The sound of glass crackled in my ears. Golden Gloves's arms dropped to his side.

The crowd booed and cheered. Everything went so slow and fast and I don't know how I knew but nothing was right about what Bobby "Golden Gloves" Dragon was in the ring with. 'Cause Death had come to fight.

And Death would win.

The crowd roAAARRRED!

12

"FREEZE!" said the cops on bullhorns, and everybody in the warehouse scattered like cockroaches when the overhead lights came on.

Mama grabbed my hand and flung me toward Richie like a dollie. "Go with him," Mama said.

But I was froze. Golden Gloves lay there in the center of the ring. He wasn't even twitching no more like he was a couple of minutes before.

"Hurry," Mama said, shaking me.

Tío Tony rushed over to Pape like some kinda

superhero and lifted him right outta his chair. They disappeared in the crowd scrambling and stomping all over each other to get away from the cops waving their batons and guns.

"Come on," Richie barked. "Faster."

Richie shoved and kicked his way through an endless wall of people, pulling me behind him.

El Jefe? Where had he gone?

Richie swung me round a corner and down a long hall that was so dark I could only see him in splashes of light. There were people running ahead of us. Quick bursts of light at the end of that forever hallway. I could hear people scrambling from a distance. Sirens squealing.

I looked back and saw dots of light bounce behind us almost becoming beams.

"The police," I said to Richie.

Richie looked back and pulled me harder.

Richie told me once how he'd run in bad with a couple of white cops. How he wasn't doing nothing but standing and this pig cracked him in the gut. My gut was a lot softer than Richie's. It would hurt me a lot more.

"Andale, Chula."

My feet were all heavy but I wasn't gonna

drop like those dumb white girls in scary movies. Like why were they always alone in the dark in movies? That was dumb. At least I had Richie, even if he seemed scared too.

We made it to the end of the hall and Richie blew through the doors. But we came out the back not the front and were fenced in. Three guys dropped off the other side of the fence and ran. Richie didn't think twice and cat-climbed up the chain fence. I stood glued to the ground. At the top, he looked down.

"¿Qué pasó?" he asked.

I couldn't do it.

"Don't be afraid," said Richie.

But I was. When I was seven, I tried climbing a fence and fell and broke my right arm. I could feel my arm tingle at the thought of getting up there. The echo of footsteps getting closer didn't make things better. My heart rocketed.

"You won't fall," said Richie.

I just kept shaking my head. He swung his leg over to leave me, then hung there. I started crying 'cause I knew how much softer my gut was than Richie's. It would hurt.

Richie rocked back and forth. "Dammit,

Chula." He threw his leg back over and came down. "Go. If you drop, I'll catch you. Please, Chula."

What about the time he flung me off a trampoline and laughed and laughed as I lay crying on the ground? Would he really catch me? There wasn't a whole lotta time to figure it out. I fastened my fingers to the fence, shaking and sweaty. That thing was at least ten feet high.

"Hurry, Chula."

I stuck my foot in a hole and climbed. My stomach must of swole up into my throat from being so scared. I was halfway there and Richie said, "You can do it. Don't give up."

At the top, I flung my leg over, straddling the fence like a seesaw. It waved back and forth all loose. Suddenly my head got light and I thought I was gonna fall, or worse, puke.

"Ay dios mio, Richie. I'm scared, I swear it I am."

For the first time, I admitted a weakness to my mean and selfish brother.

"You're almost there," he said.

The sound of shoes was getting closer.

"Swing your other leg over. Come on, Chula.

Mama will be pissed you stay up there like you're a little bird."

I couldn't help but smile and he smiled too. My arms shook real hard, limbs in a huge gust of wind, as I pushed up and over. The toes of my sneakers fit snug in the fence holes again.

"That's it," Richie said as I eased down.

Just as I sprang off the fence Richie shot off the ground to climb it. But there wasn't enough Monkey Blood in him yet 'cause two cops came charging up behind him. He climbed faster but they flung him back, ripping his shirt.

"Run, Chula!" shouted Richie.

They grabbed him real hard and threw him down on his belly.

"Run," he said, and I did.

I ran and ran and looked back hoping that Richie might've squirmed away but there was nothing but street behind me. Maybe he did some fancy move like on the karate video games he liked playing so much. Or maybe El Jefe emerged from the darkness of the warehouse and pounced on the cops like they were grapes. Like small stupid little things.

What scared me the most was thinking what

two pigs would do with a Mexican trying to get away from them. But for the first time in I couldn't remember, in forever, I did exactly what my stupid mean older brother said. I ran.

It seemed like hours till I made it home. I shot through the back door.

Mama and Pape sat in the living room. Prayer candles lit all over the place.

"Where's your brother?" Mama asked all worried.

"I dunno."

"Mi'jita, por favor," she said. "¿Dónde está Richie?"

"I dunno. He help me climb a fence. I was scared so he waited for me to make it over. The police came. . . ."

Mama's face grew empty and her eyes swole with tears.

"He says to me to run so I did," I said.

Pape sat quiet with his hand propping up his chin. Everything was all bad. Not only was Richie in trouble but Golden Gloves had to be hurt bad not to be moving or nothing.

"Go to bed," said Mama.

"But . . . we have to help Richie."

"What more are you gonna do, Chula?" asked Mama.

"Elena," said Pape.

"Stay out of this, Hector. We have nothing now and no way to help Richie. Everything was on this fight–"

"I know what was on the fight," he yelled.

"And now because of . . ." And Mama caught herself.

I knew what she wanted to say without her even looking too far in my direction. I had been her favorite till the accident. Then she had to put all her love for Pape and me somewhere. She had to have a shoulder to cry on and someone to tell her sadness to who wasn't a priest 'cause they might look down on her. She needed Richie to be everything that Pape and me wasn't. Without Richie, then what? What would we do with the fight raided and the money gone and knowing there wouldn't be any fights for months, if ever?

Mama lit another candle.

I went around the corner to my room and saw a flickering yellow-white glow from the crack in Richie's door. I put my eye against the crack and saw a prayer candle almost burnt out on Richie's nightstand. El Jefe sat on the end of the bed in his glittery red and gold trunks. His giant shadow waved like a flag on the wall and leapt onto the ceiling like it was trying to fly away from him. His hands still taped from the fight held his face up. Then I heard a sound. A soft . . . crying.

What kind of monster cried?

13

"Get up!" Mama said standing in the door. "You're late, Chula."

I pulled the blanket over my head. Her heels smacked on the floor and she snapped the covers off of me.

"Now," she said.

At least it was Friday.

I sat down at the kitchen table. A plate of cold chorizo taquitos already waiting. Abuela hunched over her plate, smiling all kidlike as she picked the pieces of pepper out of her taquito.

"No, Abuela," said Mama in the softest voice I ever heard her use.

Mama folded the taquito closed.

"Do you know me?" asked Abuela to Mama.

"Yes, Abuela," said Mama. "I know you very well."

"Will you tell me who I am?"

Mama looked over at me staring. Pape would be up soon. Seeing Abuela like that would break his heart. Mama reached over to the radio and slipped in a cassette tape. The most beautiful Spanish music came on. Very classy. Nothing tejano or fast about it. The man's voice sounded kinda sad but it made Abuela so happy. She didn't ask us questions when she heard his voice. Mama didn't want Abuela to ask Pape what she'd just asked her, especially that morning.

I bit into my breakfast, gagging on the store-bought tortilla.

"Stop making those faces, Chula," said Mama, making Pape's breakfast. "There are children starving in Iraq."

There were children starving in our house for hand-rolled tortillas.

I poured a cup of milk, reading the front page of the newspaper:

ILLEGAL PRIZEFIGHT LEAVES LOCAL DEAD

"Ay dios mio," said Mama, flipping over the paper. "Eat your breakfast. That's for your father."

She leaned out the kitchen doorway. "Hector, your breakfast is ready."

"He's dead, Mama," I said.

"Pues, I can read, Chula. Now eat."

"I don't see why I gotta go to school," I said. "I need to be here."

She pulled the phone book off the top of the fridge.

"El Jefe going to jail?" I asked.

"You can't go to jail if you don't exist. As far as America goes, he don't exist."

Mama popped the pages of the phone book.

"Richie exists," I said.

"He's young. Thankfully," she said.

"Did you already call that lawyer, Ralph?" I asked.

"He's in jail too." She picked up the cordless phone. "The luck of this family."

She started leaving messages with lawyers. I turned the newspaper back over.

Twenty-two people were arrested in the Thursday night raid. The Westcove police released a statement: "We are still searching for the man who fought and killed Robert Dragon, the Golden Gloves champion. We have no credible leads at this time." A service will be held for Robert Dragon Sunday at Thomas Funeral Home. He is survived by parents, Joe and Carol Dragon of Westcove, and brother, Kyle, of Austin, Texas. Dragon was 19 and expected to box professionally at the end of the year.

"Hey." Mama covered the receiver. "Take your pills and go. I'm not writing you an excuse."

I didn't have one pill all day the day before and nothing, I mean nada happened. Not one spin and not one twitch. Nothing. Maybe I didn't really need them at all. Maybe it was like the Monkey's Blood and I had enough in me. I mean, I made it over that fence. I outran the police.

Maybe I really was getting stronger.

"Now," said Mama.

She went back to the phone. "Yes, mam. I'm sorry. . . ."

Abuela reached across the table and held my hand. Her skin felt like warm cotton. She smiled at me with a mouth full of food.

"I'll see you after school, Abuela," I said, pushing my chair back.

She patted my hand and watched me until I was gone.

I walked past Pape's room as he made the bed. It took him like ten minutes and it never came out the way he wanted. Still he did it every morning. I watched his big hands struggle to smooth out the creases. His hands . . .

His hands were on the wheel. I can remember that.

"The light, Pape," I shouted, but we went right through.

His knuckles squeezed white. My stomach in my throat or my eyes or somewhere I don't know 'cause we were moving so fast. There was a car. We swerved—spun—

I just remember spinning. And glass. There was so much glass.

I skipped my pills, grabbed my books off the couch and left for school. Only I wasn't expecting for nothing to run into Freddy Cortez just a couple of blocks from the house.

"Where's your brother?" asked Freddy.

"Where do you think?" I said real smart.

He grabbed my arm and I could feel it bruising. "I'm not playing around with you," he said. "And your bodyguard isn't here to make me let go."

"He got picked up," I said. "I swear it. Last night at the fight."

He flung me loose. My arm throbbed.

"I didn't see him there," said Freddy.

"You think he wouldn't go? Everyone went," I said.

Freddy rubbed his chin. "Your parents gonna get him out?"

"I dunno. Like we're broke," I said. "Can I go now?"

Freddy watched me real close. His cell phone rang. He looked at the screen, then at me.

"Your brother gets out, tell him we're on tonight," Freddy said. "Don't forget."

Freddy stepped to the side answering his

phone. Like I'd be forgetting him the way he squeezed my freakin' arm. Cabrón.

Jo and Mary Alice bombarded me the minute I hit the junior high hallway. They'd seen the paper and that was all their mothers talked about on the phone that morning. They got right up on me chirping in my ear and I had to hush them 'cause they got too loud.

"Is it true that they picked up Richie?" asked Mary Alice.

I nodded, pushing my way to my locker.

"What about . . ." Mary Alice lowered her voice. "Did *he* run off?"

"You know, my mom says if there's a reward she's gonna tell the police he's been staying with you," said Jo.

"You can go tell your mom my mom will kick her back to Tampico if she goes and does that," I said with a growling stare.

"What you say about my mom?" Jo snapped.

For the first time, I actually didn't look away when Jo challenged me.

"Hey, calm down," Mary Alice said, separating me and Jo.

I got my algebra book out and slammed my locker shut. They just stared at me.

"What?" I asked, annoyed.

"We're your best friends, Chula," said Mary Alice. "We just want to know what happened, that's all."

"Yeah, what's the big deal, Mexican?" asked Jo. "I mean, we won last night."

Jo grinned at Mary Alice.

"Golden Gloves is dead," I said. "That ain't winning, Jo."

Jo called out my name but I kept walking down the hall. I passed Richie's dumb-head Dark Skin friends leaning up against the lockers. Their squinty eyes following me. Pendejos.

I sank into my desk chunking my ragged book under it. First things first, quizzes handed back. I got mine and almost screamed.

EXCELLENT!

Slapped in red across the top of my paper. B–! B– was almost a B and a B was almost a B+ which was like I got an A.

Yippee! I wasn't a retard long-eye. I had never been excellent at math before and I had to double-check that it was my name at the top. Yep. That was me. Chula Sanchez. Chula Sanchez was EX-CELLENT! for the first time in seventh grade.

When Mr. Maskin handed out the new quiz, I smiled real big and even got up to sharpen my pencil. Jo looked at me like "What's got you so happy?" but she couldn't bring me down 'cause I was excellent and it was the best I'd felt in a really long time. Well, except for talking to El Jefe that day at the Playground but that was different.

I sat back down at my desk and concentrated as hard as I could. I wanted another one of those excellents bad!

14

Me and Mary Alice were in the food line starving like crazy 'cause we been looking for Jo when Jo cut, pissing off everybody behind us.

"Where were you?" I asked her.

"Nowhere. Man, this is gross," Jo said, looking at the food. "How much more gringafied can this get?"

The lunch ladies loaded our trays with overcooked peas, sticky steak fingers and lumpy mashed potatoes. Two cartons of skim milk that if it didn't get any cooler outside I'd be puking up after PE.

"I bet you on Cinco de Mayo next year they'll have us eating fish sticks and Jell-O," said Jo.

Before we got to the end to pay, Ross the Floss bumped against me on his way out of the cafeteria and dropped a note on my tray. Jo and Mary Alice didn't see the note and I don't think Carla did either. But Carla saw me sharing the same freakin' air with her little brother for like two seconds too long. I tried acting like it was nothing and dug into my jeans for my free lunch card, hiding the note at the same time. Jo saw me looking over in Royal Rich and her eyes narrowed 'cause both Carla and Mitzy were looking at me all ugly.

"Jo, don't do her nothing," I said. "You just got outta I.S.S."

The lunch ladies handed us our cards and we made for Tan Land but Carla and Mitzy were there to cut us off. Jo's head cocked back . . . way back, but Carla's eyes fixed on me.

"I told you to stay away from my brother, Messy-can."

"Callate el ocico, gringa," said Jo.

"Sorry, I don't speak Mexican," said Carla.

Mary Alice stepped up. Mary Alice never stepped up.

"It's *Spanish,* pendeja," Mary Alice said. "Since we don't speak racist-white-girl you should probably stop talking to us. ¿Comprende?"

I swished my head to Jo who hadn't moved an inch, but her fist was as tight as it could be without her nails making her palms bleed.

Carla pointed her bony crooked finger at me. "Just stay away—"

And before she could finish, Jo's tray smashed onto the floor and she had Carla's bony finger bent back. So freakin' back that Carla twisted around yalping, trying to get loose. Mitzy was so stunned she stood there just looking back at Royal Rich for reinforcements. They weren't moving.

"Jo . . . ," I said. "Jo, stop."

Jo dropped Carla's finger and looked at me like I was crazy. Completely off my chain!

Carla spun around with mascara streaking from where she had cried, and spit in Jo's face. "Filthy Messy-can."

I shoved her then with Mary Alice right behind me and someone shoved me, smashing mashed potatoes all over my shirt. The kids went to chanting, "Fight! Fight! Fight!" and no way did I feel powerful. No way did I want to hear any of them say my name.

Outside the principal's office, they had Mexicans on one bench, gringas on another. They called all our parents. If I was lucky, maybe the phone had got cut off again.

Carla came out of Mr. Shannon's office nursing her hand with an ice pack. She wasn't really hurt, big faker. I knew I wasn't gonna get off like I did two days before 'cause Mr. Shannon wasn't an easy man. He was bald on purpose and useta be in the marines. "I run a tight ship," he said the first day of school over the intercom. "You get out of line, you get the paddle."

He was famous for his paddle. They say it was as thick as a history book and when he swung it, he *swung* it. I'd seen tough guys, angry I'll-bite-through-concrete guys came out of Mr. Shannon's office crying.

"Dolores," Mr. Shannon said, standing in his door.

"Chula," I said standing. "Dolores is my middle name."

The door clicked behind me and the blinds clapped against it. I sat down with my eyes already scanning for the paddle.

"Chewa-la," said Mr. Shannon. "You know, you're close to finishing off the year in lower-level classes. I've got your file right here." He pounded his finger on a folder. "Do you understand what I'm saying?"

He paused real long between words, being careful to pronounce them just right. What was wrong with that gringo?

"Right. Well, I couldn't get ahold of your mother, so you'll sit in I.S.S for the rest of the day—"

"I.S.S.? But I didn't do—"

"And you're expected to come to Saturday class."

Oh, my God! Saturday class? That was like worse than electric shock treatment, not that I'd had it but my tío Robert from the Valley did and he's never been right after. Saturday class!

"You and your friends can't go picking fights in the lunchroom. I'm aware of what happened on Wednesday and from the look on your face I can see you were an active participant."

I started nodding real angry. "She came to our

table," I said. "She started saying stuff—pointing her finger. We're not dogs they can just go and kick when they feel like it."

"Did she say something derogatory to you?" Mr. Shannon asked.

I had NO idea what that meant but she probably did do it 'cause she so mean.

"Look, Chewa-la. Part of life is learning to get along with our peers no matter what our differences are. I mean, the President of the United States doesn't beat up the President of Germany just because they don't see eye to eye on foreign policy. There are other ways to work things out."

I didn't pay much attention to the news so I couldn't really argue what the president does or doesn't do. I knew he didn't give us no tax break 'cause Mama go to groaning about it every April.

"Do you understand?" he asked.

He did that slow talking thing again, so I just kept my eyes down 'cause if I looked at him I might've said something that would've got me in a whole lotta trouble. Things weren't looking so good already.

He reached in his desk and my butt started to

tense up. Not the paddle. Not that paddle. He pulled out . . . a bright yellow slip of paper.

"Give this to your mother," he said. "Have her sign it and set up a meeting with me."

He walked me to the door. "You know, Chewa-la," he said, "you can turn this all around."

Sitting in In School Suspension was probably a lot worse than jail. In jail, they let you eat somewhere else and have exercise. I.S.S. meant you were staple-gunned to your chair and were allowed to go to the bathroom twice a day. Once in the morning and once in the afternoon. Only if your aunt Rosa was visiting, as Mama called your monthly, then you could go more. My aunt Rosa hadn't even thought about visiting yet and the first thing I done when I got to I.S.S. was pee.

I sat there in the three-walled desk reading about these hollow men and how they got heads made of straw. Poetry was soooooo confusing. I had to reread a stanza like three times. Then I remembered Ross the Floss's note. I raised up a little to make sure Coach Jones was still sitting behind the desk. I was in enough trouble without getting busted reading a note.

I dug the note out of my pocket and unfolded it real quiet.

Chula,

I'm really sorry I got you in trouble with Carla. I didn't mean for you to get it from her I swear. I really need to talk to you. I don't know who else to talk to. Let me know and we can meet somewhere outside school if you want. I hope you write soon.

Sincerely,

Ross Johnson

The three-thirty bell rang. I shot up outta my seat, shoving the note in my back pocket. Jo and Mary Alice popped outta their seats and sped for the door.

"Walk," said Coach Jones. "You run on the field."

Richie would've said, "If you Mexican, you run every second of your life."

I wasn't outta I.S.S. two seconds and Jo swooped in.

"So what's the deal?" she asked. "Why you telling me to lay off Carla when she step to us? I mean what, you're sweet on her brother or something?"

"What?"

148

"All I'm saying is we always back you but if you're running with gringos like that"–Jo looked to Mary Alice who wanted to stay out of it–"well, I just don't know."

"First off, like I said, I ain't sweet on nobody. Second, we're supposed to be friends no matter what. I mean like, you sound like one of them racists."

Jo stood with her head still as far back as it would go but you could see she didn't like calling me out like that. The three of us, we were family. A family that hated not getting along.

"Who's got enough for ice cream?" asked Mary Alice.

Jo dug in her baggy jeans pocket and pulled out a buck. I had the same. We were all starving and could've each eat a banana split but when we got to the Sonic, we shared one. With extra nuts and whipped topping. Nobody brought up El Jefe or Richie. Not even Carla calling us Messy-cans, which I knew burnt all of us real good. We talked about Mary Alice's party that was next Saturday and how everybody was gonna come and how it was gonna be so fun. We talked like we were really saying something only we weren't. We weren't saying nothing at all and for the first time in knowing them, that kinda bothered me.

15

I stood outside Tía Josie's door. I had never stood at her door in my whole life. I played with Esperanza in elementary only 'cause Mama couldn't be there to tell me no. I even got to talk to Tía Josie sometimes when she picked Esperanza up from school. But I'd never been there at that door. At the door with a welcome mat that didn't say nothing. It just had faded flowers circling a basket of fruit.

I pushed the doorbell. No one came. I opened the screen door and knocked. My heart raced, which was all kinds of crazy. She was my tía. No matter what Mama said about her she was still family. There was nothing to be nervous about.

Tía opened the door. Her smile lit me all up inside.

"Chula," she said. "Come in."

Coming to the door was one thing but going in . . . going in and being seen coming out would have me grounded till high school. But I went in anyway.

The walls were so alive with color. Bright beautiful colors like the way Pape had always spoke of Mexico. There were framed pictures of deserts and famous faraway places but most of the pictures were of Esperanza. Pictures on the tables and the entertainment center. In the bookcases and on the walls. After the accident I only really remembered things like how she useta laugh or say "See ya." But in all those pictures there was this kinda light in her eyes that I'd forgotten about.

"Can I get you something? Iced tea? A Coke?"

My eyes lit up. "A Pepsi?"

"I'll check." She went into the kitchen. "You're

in luck. One can of Pepsi left. Do you want a glass?"

"No, that's okay. Your house is really nice, Tía," I said looking at all of her books. "It's bigger than it looks from the street."

She handed me the can.

"You read all these books?" I said.

"Yeah. I love to read. What about you?"

"I useta but after the accident . . . sometimes it's just hard," I said, sipping the Pepsi. "But I'm in accelerated classes this year."

"The college track. That's great, Chula. I'm actually starting college next fall."

"College? For real?" I asked all shocked.

"I've been saving up for a long time. First for Espi, but then after she died I just kept saving not really knowing why. Until a few months ago. You wanna sit down?"

I took off my backpack and plopped on her soft couch. She sat in a chair beside me.

"What's wrong, Chula?"

"Tía, I need a favor. And I'm the last person who should be asking for favors from you, but–"

"Chula, your mother and I don't get along but if you need something, I'll help you any way I can."

I'd rehearsed what I'd say the minute I left Jo and Mary Alice at the Sonic. But right then, it all sounded so stupid in my head.

"Just tell me," she said.

"The family's in trouble. Big time."

"How much did they bet on the fight?"

"Everything. And even worse, Richie got picked up. I don't know what we'll do. Mama makes so little working at the bakery and Pape can't do nothing. Can you help us, Tía?"

"What did your mother say?"

I dropped my head. "Couldn't you just give me the money?" I asked. "I would say I found it."

"Mi'jita, I can't do that."

"But she'll never take it from you."

"But she'll risk your and Richie's safety with that monster in her house?"

"Don't say that." I set the Pepsi on the coffee table.

She reached for my hands. "It's true."

"No. You're wrong about him." I pushed her hands off. "Everyone thinks he meant it but he didn't. I seen him cry. What kind of monster cries, Tía?" I picked up my backpack. "I gotta go before Mama thinks I've been taken by the devil, or worse by gringos."

Tía dropped her head.

"I'm sorry. . . . I didn't mean it like that," I said. "I think it's dumb. That she's all mad 'cause of seeds."

"Ay, mi'jita. It's not just about seeds. I don't know what your mother has told you."

Nothing I wanted to be repeating.

"See, I was just thirteen when my sister met your father. And a few months later she turned eighteen and got married and left our abuela's house. But my abuela got to where she couldn't take care of me, so I went to live with your parents and your abuela. Your mother loved me so much then."

It was like Tía Josie was somewhere else. Somewhere so far I couldn't make it up.

"She worked two jobs. Even after Richie was born, she made sure I had everything. She made sacrifices for me, Chula. Sacrifices that I couldn't have understood when I was seventeen and telling her how I would keep the baby and not go to Princeton. You should've seen her. She was as swollen as me with you in her belly but still offered to raise Esperanza so I'd go to college."

I couldn't believe Mama would ever offer to have a gringo of any kind live in her house.

"And as scared as I was—and I *was scared*—I knew I had to raise Esperanza. And your mother felt like everything she'd done to get me out of the Circle was for nothing."

"But didn't you wanna get out?" I said.

"Of course mi'jita. But there's always another way." She smiled softly. "That much I learned from your father."

I stayed quiet.

"Chula, I want to help you. If my sister or your father would take money from me, I'd give it in a second. But they have to take it from me, no lying. I know you know that."

"Yeah," I said, slinging my backpack over my shoulder.

I walked over to the front door with her behind me.

"Chula, stop by again. Okay?"

I nodded and walked out.

I came in the front door and heard voices in the kitchen. Mama, Pape, Tío Tony and . . . I came around the corner.

"You bust out," I said to Richie.

He leaned on the counter with a mouthful of sandwich. I ran right up and hugged him. I think he felt weird about it but he hugged me anyway.

"Man, I thought you gonna pee your pants on that fence," Richie said laughing.

"Shut up, pendejo," I said, putting my backpack down. "They should've kept you longer."

"Chula," Mama snapped. "You want to go to bed without dinner?"

I smelled beef and cheese enchiladas baking in the oven. No way was I going anywhere empty-bellied that night.

"How'd you get out?" I asked Richie.

"They had to let me go," Richie said, opening the fridge. " 'Cause I don't know anything."

He pulled out a pitcher of sweet tea.

"And 'cause he's going to court next week, where he'll probably end up doing *a lot* more community service," said Mama. "If we are all lucky."

"What do you mean if we're lucky?" I asked.

"The police wanted to know how I could've let him be there," said Mama.

Richie rolled his eyes at her.

"Don't roll your eyes at me," she said. "They could put you in a foster home. It could happen."

"Mama," he said, kissing her forehead. "They're not after me. They're after El Jefe."

"He's right, Elena," Tío Tony said. He stood up and put his coffee cup in the sink. "I need to get going. Richie, stay out of trouble."

Richie slap-shook his hand. "Thanks for bailing me out."

"Yeah well, don't forget. You show up to the garage after school starting Monday for the next two weeks."

"He won't forget," said Pape.

Richie rolled his eyes.

"Hector, I'll give you a call about moving El Jefe," Tío Tony said.

Pape nodded with his chin leaning on his fingertips as Tío slipped out the back door.

"Moving him where?" I asked.

"Ay, Chula," Mama said annoyed. "You have so many questions. How can you wonder so much?"

She got up from the table and stood over the stove.

Richie leaned in and said to me, "They're

hot to find El Jefe. It would've been one thing if Bobby D. was Mexican. Case closed. But a Golden Gloves white boy? They'll juice El Jefe for sure."

"Richie," said Pape.

"What?" asked Richie. "She's old enough to know what's going on."

"Enough," said Pape.

"Hector, he just got home," said Mama. "Can we please not fight tonight?"

Pape pushed himself away from the table, straining to get a chair outta his way.

"What are you doing?" said Mama to Pape. "Dinner will be ready in half an hour."

"I'm going to speak with him," Pape said. "Or would you rather I let you do that too?"

I'd never seen Pape look at Mama like that. Like he'd cut her down if she said yes.

"Bueno," Mama said, her eyes quickly falling to a skillet of rice.

I waited for Pape to wheel out of the kitchen before I asked Richie, "They really gonna juice him? It was an accident. He didn't mean to kill him."

Richie looked to Mama who waited to see how he would answer me.

"Don't worry," said Richie to me. "They'd have to find him first."

"It ain't no secret that he's here," I said.

"People in this neighborhood may talk a lot," said Mama. "But they know when to be quiet."

"So what happens?" I asked.

"He'll just have to go," said Mama. "Now enough questions."

Richie set his glass on the counter and made for the living room. I followed behind him.

"Hey, Richie."

"What, Chula?" he said all impatient, flopping on the couch.

"Where would he go?" I asked.

"Back to Mexico, I guess."

"That would make sense," I said, sitting beside him. " 'Cause they love him there."

Richie peeled the curtain back, looking between the bars on the living room window.

"Can you imagine it, Richie?" I asked. "He gets to live somewhere that they sprinkle him with holy water. And throw lilies and yellow roses and spray perfumes when he walks by. I mean, even the priests love him."

"What are you talking about?" asked Richie.

"El Jefe. How the people love him in Mexico," I said.

Richie shook his head. "Pues, he was in prison," said Richie. "You know that. No one loves him. So quit trying to make him into something special."

But I seen it. I seen magic in him kneeling at Pape's bed. And he understood things different than anybody else. And Pape, Pape said they showered El Jefe with flowers and foods and the love of all of Mexico.

"Ay, get off the couch," said Richie, stretching out. "At least I'll get my room back. Pues, this couch sucks."

"Chula," Mama said from the kitchen in her I-don't-want-any-lip voice.

"What?"

"Get in here and set the table."

I went to the kitchen and pulled the plates outta the cabinet. I was almost done setting the table when I remembered. I reached in my backpack and held the algebra quiz folded up in my hand.

"Hey, Mama, guess what?" I asked.

"Ay, Chula, I have no time for guessing."

I shoved my quiz under her nose.

"I'm excellent. Just like Tía Josie."

She shoved it outta her face.

"Well good for you. Maybe you'll get filthy seeds and move out of the house so we don't have to worry about you."

I felt like I just got punched ten times all in my soft belly. Even her not holding me since the accident wasn't as bad as what she just said.

She reached in the oven and pulled out the enchiladas. Acting like she had said nothing mean to me. Not one thing.

Even though it was Friday, Mama sent us off to do homework right after we done the dishes. I opened my history book but couldn't think about history. I propped my head on the pages, thinking about the fight and climbing the fence and if it really did hurt when Bobby Dragon died.

I wondered what El Jefe was thinking about sitting alone in Richie's room surrounded by posters of lowriders and Dr. Dre, Eminem, or whatever bad-A cool guy Richie could admire more than Pape. Did El Jefe look into the eyes of those men and understand their anger—their strength? Could he smell the enchiladas and rice still in the air from dinner over an hour earlier and wish he had a plate too? He hadn't come to dinner. As far as I knew, he hadn't come outta his room since the fight 'cept maybe to go to the bathroom when I was at school.

"You gotta read it to remember it," said Richie, chomping on a Baby Ruth in my doorway.

"Where'd you get that?" I asked.

He grinned all cool strutting in and plopped on my bed.

"I'd give you a bite but it would only make you fatter," he said.

"I ain't fat, Mexican," I said to him.

He poked at my belly. His finger hurt so I squirmed and tried slapping him but missed.

"Pretty girls don't have roly pudges like that. It's okay. Most people don't match their names."

He saw the red EXCELLENT—peeking outta my folder.

"I got it in algebra today," I said. "I bet I can get another one."

"Well, if you don't you can always get married. That's what's good about being a girl. Your husband can do the hard stuff and he won't care if you got As or not"

Richie didn't understand how dumb he sounded. Mama kept all the bills and bank straight and she was a girl. I missed the Richie that useta be kind of cool. But I couldn't tell that to the new Richie.

"Pape says you study you ain't gotta fight," I said. "You ain't got to marry and you can get out of the Circle."

"Pape says a lot of things, Chula. That's what people do when they can't do nothing else. Let me tell you something, and you remember it good. You're a Mexican and you'll always be Mexican. It ain't nothing to drop your head about but that year-round tan of yours means you'll always have to fight for what you want. Especially if you ain't got a man to do it for you," said Richie. "I sure hope you get a man, Chula. It's hard fighting."

It was the first real advice Richie ever gave me and it was the most confusing. I just wanted him to be glad I got an excellent in math.

His phone vibrated.

"What?" I asked, watching him read it.

He left the candy wrapper on my history book and went over to my window, raising it all careful so it wouldn't squeak.

"What are you doing, pendejo?" I said to him.

"Shh . . . it's Friday night."

163

Friday night meant Richie had to meet the Dark Skins at the Playground. Most of the time it was all harmless 'cause they'd get some drunk to buy them beer, or hang out on a corner hollering at hot-pants girls. But Richie had the dumbest look on his face. He looked like something was gonna happen. That was the first Friday I'd ever been scared to see him crawl outta my window and he'd done it I don't know how many times.

"Relax, Chula. . . . It's really okay."

"Richie," I said.

"What?" he said all impatient.

"Freddy come looking for you," I said.

"When?"

"This morning. On my way to school," I said, lifting my T-shirt sleeve.

My arm was bruised up bad.

"He do that to you?" Richie asked shocked.

"I smarted off."

"Y, olé," said Richie. "Just stay away from him, okay?"

And he started back out the window.

"Pues, look at my arm," I said.

"Shhh . . . ," he said. "What do you want me to do?"

"Whatever," I said.

"What?" Richie asked.

"Why you gotta run with them?"

He leaned on the window ledge. "We ain't got no money, Chula. Even the tortillas we hate from the store cost money."

"Pape's got disability," I said. "We got food stamps."

"Food stamps," Richie said, shaking his head.

Richie hated that we were on food stamps. He woulda rather not eat than have to go to the store with that Lone Star food stamp card. He woulda rather done anything than feel like that.

"I'll tell Freddy to leave you alone," said Richie.

He started to leave.

"Richie," I said. "Don't tell him nothing."

After a little bit, Richie nodded. We both knew he was no one to be telling Freddy Cortez anything about whose arm he squeezed.

"See ya," said Richie.

And he disappeared out my window just like that. The yellow curtains caught some kind of tired wind, waving, then just not moving. Not moving at all.

16

Mama stormed into my room. "Where's Richie?" she asked.

I shrugged. The window was wide open. She walked over to me. Her hand shot back without her even thinking I bet 'cause the next thing I knew my cheek was burning and I was thinking all kinds of mean things to say only I didn't 'cause I was choking on my tears.

"You're supposed to have some sense, Chula," said Mama. "Somewhere in there."

She barked at me so loud I knew the neighbors could hear.

Pape rolled in the doorway. He hated seeing girls hit more than just about anything. The day he saw Mama's brother slap her in front of him he swore no one would ever put her down again. They ran away that night with Richie cooking in her belly. Pape had planted seeds but unlike a lotta Mexican men, he wanted to see them grow.

Now he was just the lump laying beside her every night. I wondered if he didn't move if she'd forget he was even there.

"Where is Richie, Chula?"

She asked the question like the answer was somehow gonna change from every other Friday Richie slipped out. Of course she knew where he was. She only had to march down there and yank his oily black hair and say, "Mexican, get your butt home." Only she wasn't doing that like she did when Pape could back her up. Not to mention, nobody went down to the Playground after dark anymore unless they were dark enough in the heart not to be seen.

That was exactly why Richie shouldn't have been there with his machismo friends. His heart was too light. But what did I know anyway. If I had any good mind, I'd of told her outright instead of getting slapped and—

Her hand flared—

"Elena. Por favor," said Pape.

She paused. Her hand slowly went back to her side, shaking.

"Go take your medicine," she said. "Go cost us another two hundred dollars we don't have."

"Elena . . . ," said Pape.

"What, Hector?" Mama said. "Richie's right about one thing. She's old enough to know. If she even can know anything anymore." The last part Mama said more to herself but I heard.

I slipped off the bed not taking my eyes off her in case she tried to hit me again. She eased herself all slow onto my bed. Pape wheeled into the room and took her hand.

"Don't, Hector," Mama said, getting all frustrated and pushing him away.

She went to my window, shutting it like it hurt her, and just stayed there crying.

I walked to the bathroom, stopping at the door. There wasn't any sound. Not even a glow coming through the crack in Richie's door. I was sure El Jefe heard all of it. What could he think of us?

I locked the bathroom. In the mirror on the back of the door, I looked real hard at myself. My face red from Mama's hand. I slid the sleeve up on my shirt and saw Freddy's fingers pressed into my skin. No way was he gonna have my skin the way he was taking Richie's. No way was I giving him that. I was strong. I just knew it. I knew that I was excellent just like Mr. Maskin wrote.

I sat on the edge of the tub holding the two pills in my hand. My experiment was working. The less I took them the stronger I got. I hadn't had them in two whole days and nothing bad happened. No shakes, no tremors, no Flashes. And I had stood up to Jo and even Freddy Cortez and I would've never thought I could do that. What if I had gotten better? What if I could be as strong as El Jefe? So strong that Carla or Mitzy or the whole bunch of them Squares couldn't go making fun of me no more 'cause I was well. I could be in the band again and not flinch every time one of the drummers tossed me a mallet. Not think of glass breaking and shattering and sticking in my brain. I could be like everyone else and no one would remember after a while about the Flashes, about the way I talked all funny after biting my tongue, and maybe I'd even go to college like Tía Josie.

Maybe not taking those two pills really could

do all that. And just then there was a sound. Like a firecracker but deeper. Harder.

A couple of minutes later, police sirens pierced the Circle. Flashes of red and ghost white splattered across the bathroom window. Richie . . .

I raced down the hall and saw Mama and Pape looking out the living room window.

"What happened?" I asked.

Mama opened the front door. Police cars *zoooomed* through the neighborhood. "Go to your room," Mama said. "Stay away from the windows. NOW."

I ran to my bedroom, seeing Richie's door at the end of the hall. I started to go down there when I heard a noise in my window. Richie belly flopped in with blood running down his head.

"Jesus," I said. "What happen?"

He dropped all hard to the floor, pulling one of my curtains down with him.

"Where's El Jefe?" asked Richie.

"What?"

"El Jefe? Is he here? He has to hide."

I grabbed one of my T-shirts and handed it to Richie.

"Put this on your head," I said.

He poured down with sweat like he came right out of a hot shower. There was a loud KNOCK on the front door. A banging.

"What did you do, Mexican?" I asked whispering.

"I run," he said. "I just run."

Richie was bleeding like crazy from his head and Mama was at the door talking to cops 'cause I heard voices over a radio-CB thing that cops carry.

"You gotta hide, Richie," I said.

I hooked under his arm and pulled his skinny-heavy body up.

"Ay, help me, man," I whispered.

"Ay, something hurts," he said, grabbing his side.

"Sh. Everything's gonna hurt if the pigs find you. Come on."

I buried him in the closet under my two weeks of laundry. I stacked sneakers and flats, a big blue-jean jacket and two sweatshirts on him. He almost couldn't breathe, maybe 'cause there was so much stuff all over him. Then I ran to my bed and scooped up all the dollies and stuffed animals and chunked them on top of him. I went to close the door and he said from below the pile, "Gracias, Chula."

"Shut up or they find you," I said, even though I wanted to say I'm glad you didn't go get killed but no ways was I gonna say that. Especially if he made it out of this 'cause he was gonna owe me forever.

Mama knocked on the door and opened it before I could say like anything. Behind her stepped in two big cops. One brown and one white and it didn't matter 'cause they both pigs and pigs always looking for a Mexican to roll.

"Mi'jita, these men are here looking for Richie. Where did you say your brother is?" She smiled but I knew it meant LIE.

"He go out to the movies in Square—in Westcove."

Squaretown got a name only it don't really fit.

"How did he get there?" said the brown officer.

"He took the bus," said Mama. "Our car is broke down."

Pape wheeled into the doorway and the cops glanced back at him, sizing him up as no threat.

The brown cop knelt down to me like I was some little girl he had a candy for. "Are you sure you haven't seen him in the last hour or so?" he asked.

Is this Mexican kidding me with his poster-boy smile of Colgate whites? He don't want to help us. None of us. Coconut.

"I ain't seen my brother since he go to the movies. That's the truth."

"What happened to your curtains?" asked the white cop.

The brown pig drew his smile in. "Let's take a look around," he said.

Oh my God, a look around! Richie in the closet and El Jefe down the hall. This was all bad, very, very bad.

"Don't you need a search warrant to go through our home?" Pape said, wheeling himself in.

I took his place in the doorway as the white cop explained things.

I moved real slow out of my doorway. The distance from Richie's room to mine seemed longer than usual. Had El Jefe heard the pigs come in? Was he just sitting there waiting for them to take him? Maybe he didn't think like Richie to go out the window. . . . Could he even fit?

I twisted the knob quick, springing the door

open. "Hey," shouted the brown cop from my doorway. "What are you doing?"

The raised window caught the curtain in this whipping motion and there was a

FLASH

17

i came to on the floor with some gringo flashing a light in my eye. I tried to get up but my arms started to shake. I saw Mama and she was real scared and crying.

"It's okay, Chula. You're okay, mi'jita," Mama said. "Just be still."

I raised my sore neck. Pape was to my other side laying on the floor holding my head down.

"Be still, Chulita," said Pape.

Chulita?

Breathing felt real hard and that gringo put a

mask over my nose and mouth and it didn't seem much better.

"Don't panic," said the gringo. "You're hyper-ventilating. Calm down."

"Mama?" I said muffled.

"You just fell down, mi'jita," she said.

I tried to figure what she meant when it finally hit me.

"No . . . ," I said through tears and my swollen tongue. "No Flashes. I'm strong—strong like Jefe."

I tried to get up more determined but my muscles wouldn't let me as they went all wobbly. The gringo gripped my shoulders to ease me back down.

"Have you skipped doses of your medication?" asked the gringo.

The last thing I wanted to do was admit that. I'd be grounded past Mary Alice's party, past my own birthday in June. I'd be yelled at and maybe even slapped 'cause another ambulance bill would set us back and there wasn't no further back for us to go. I didn't know how to answer so I just nodded.

Mama was crushed and left the hall. I started crying all big and hard and Pape brushed my sweaty hair from my forehead.

He leaned real close to my ear and said, "Shhh . . . think about Mexico. The colores. The smells of mangos and bananas and las raspadas dripping down your arm . . ."

Abuela had stepped in. She stood over me and her smile was so warm. Pape's voice became her voice and the Spanish sounded like music. Like flavor. Like my heart beating.

I must've stopped crying at some point and fallen off to sleep 'cause when I woke up a little after two a.m. I had no idea how I got from the hall to my bed and in fresh clothes. I looked over at the closet and the pile of clothes was all strung out in these clumps. The dollies scattered on the floor like lost childen at the grocery. Then something moved on the bed and I strained to turn my sore neck. It was Richie. Cuddled up, sleeping.

Where was El Jefe?

I didn't wake up until one-something Saturday afternoon. It felt like I'd just got done from eight hours of wall sits and push-ups the way my muscles were all tired and hurting. Richie sat on the end of my bed just staring.

"What?" I asked, struggling to push myself up.

"The school called this morning," he said.

"They told Mama you were supposed to be in Saturday class."

"Ay," I said, knowing I was in all kinds of trouble with Mama. "She get all mad?"

He shook his head. "Think she was too tired to get mad. She told them what happened to you last night. They said you could do it next weekend." He kept staring.

"Man did you snore last night, Chula. Real loud that the walls almost crack."

"Shut up," I said.

I reached in my nightstand drawer and pulled out a mirror. My eye was almost back to normal but my lip was gonna scar. And my tongue. Now that was gross. All chewed and puffy.

"What happened?" I asked. "When I Flashed?"

"The cops were in here nosing around and I was sure I'd get busted. Then I heard one of them yell at you and . . ." Richie's voice got kind of low. "Mama started screaming like crazy. And Pape went after her and I heard him push himself right out of that chair onto the floor with you. If you can believe it. The cops were so busy getting the ambulance they forgot about me, so I lay there like forever, man. Totally needing to go, you know."

"Yeah . . . ," I said, knowing exactly.

"I could hear you," said Richie. "Your shoes were just beating on the floor."

"It ain't like I meant to," I said.

"Did I say you did?" he asked all frustrated. "It's just . . . Pues, I don't know. Scary that you could die like that."

Richie never talked about the Flashes. I figured he didn't care what happened and maybe even wished I'd died in that car wreck instead of embarassing him with getting sick. I had no idea what to say to him, so we both stayed quiet.

"So, why you come in here all busted up last night?" I asked.

"Freddy wanted a couple of us to hold up the grocery next to Tiny's Video."

"You robbed some place?" I asked.

"Y, olé, calm down," he said. "We went down there and stood in the alley. Freddy handed us these Halloween masks—"

"What was yours?" I asked.

"A clown."

"Figures," I said.

"You wanna know or not?" he asked. "So we're about to go in when Ruben's gang pulls up and spots us. Ruben started telling stuff to Freddy and Freddy hits Ruben and . . ."

Richie sprang off the bed and started imitating the fight, where of course he was *Matrix* kung fu times ten gazillion. Right . . . but it was his story and my body hurt too much to go getting up.

"Then Mr. Padron from across the street comes out of the store," said Richie. "And he calls my name to see if it's me–"

"How did he know who you was?" I asked.

"What? Pues, I done pulled the mask off. Pay attention," said Richie. "Anyways, he sees it's me and that I might be hurt but I go to running 'cause Freddy pulled a gun and started poppin' caps like some kinda video game."

Richie's mind drifted.

"What?" I asked.

"Sometimes I just wanna keep going, you know?" he asked. "Like when I took off from the alley, I thought, what would it be like to keep going? No Circle. No Square."

"The earth's round, pendejo," I said. "One big circle."

It seemed to hurt him what I said.

180

"So you didn't steal nothing?" I asked.

"No, retard. I just got in a fight," he said, falling back onto the bed.

"I ain't no retard, Richie."

He smiled all big. "I know."

Then I remembered. . . .

"Where's El Jefe?" I asked panicked. "I open the door and—"

"Gone," said Richie.

He couldn't be. I didn't get to say nothing to him. Not even goodbye.

"Pape had already hid him before I got here," Richie said. "They had to find a way to get him out of town without drawing attention to him. And it's a good thing 'cause there's pictures all over the TV and in the paper today. Someone snuck a camera into the fight. Here, check it out."

Richie reached into his back pocket and unfolded the picture he ripped outta the paper. It was El Jefe standing over Golden Gloves lying on the mat. The referee with his hand against El Jefe's chest. El Jefe looked so small. How could something so big look so small?

"So he went back to Mexico?" I asked. "Richie . . ."

"I don't know. Pape ain't said nothing all day.

Just been sitting with Abuela in her room. I mean, where else would El Jefe go?"

"What? What are you not saying?" I asked.

"They say on TV, they say they got a bunch of border patrol and cops looking for him. So I don't know how he'd get back in."

"I have to find him," I said, flinging the blanket back.

"Are you loco? No way, Chula. Besides, Mama ain't gonna let you outta the house."

"You don't understand, Richie," I said. "He's . . ."

And I had no idea how to tell Richie that the only person in the world that got me was a murderer. A murderer of children no less, but still he was . . . my friend.

"Chula," Richie said. "He's already gone. If not to Mexico, somewhere."

Richie reached in his pocket and pulled out one pink and a blue.

"Don't go being forgetful anymore, okay?" said Richie. He leaned beside the bed and popped open a can of Pepsi. "And don't tell Mama or she'll have my butt."

"Where's Mama?" I asked, swallowing the pills even though I didn't wanna.

He dropped his eyes getting ready to lie. I knew 'cause he did this eyebrow-rubbing thing when he was about to lay something on thick.

"Like don't even start," I said. "She don't wanna see me."

"She's just scared . . . and mad," said Richie.

Of course she was. I'd messed everything up again. Me and Pape, the ruiners of everything. Why didn't she just let them take me to the hospital and give me away to some institution? My eyes got all wet.

"Don't cry, Chula," said Richie.

But like I didn't care if he saw 'cause it wasn't fair.

"It doesn't matter if I'm excellent or not. She hates me, Richie." The words shook through the tears. "I meant to snap the belt on right. I meant to."

Richie scooted to the headboard and sat beside me. "Lift up," he said.

I looked at him like he was crazy.

"Ay, come on. I ain't gonna do you nothing."

I raised up and he slid his arm under my head and tucked me in like a baby bird under his wing. He didn't try to get me in a headlock or nothing. He just held me.

How Richie and me went from being real mean to real nice to real mean after the accident kinda made sense. He wanted me to be on his side about how Pape was wrong to drink and drive and how I should hate him as much as he did. But I forgave Pape even if he was the reason my brain got all swole and I lost a lot of memories from growing up. Even though there was so much glass not accounted for at the accident and I still think it made its way into my head forever.

"The earth's round," Richie said, like thinking it out loud for the first time. "Isn't it?"

"Yeah," I said. "It is."

In my sleep that Saturday, I dreamt of Mexico. Of the warm smell of pan dulce, and the taste of tamales, of mangos . . . of love. People lined the streets holding out these platters full of food, smiling and chanting, "Jefe! Jefe! Jefe!"

They vanished into darkness. Not like night. Darker. Footsteps moved closer. The sound of dirt breaking beneath boots. Then El Jefe stepped out of a darkness without walls without faces into lights. Bright bright lights only on him. His skin swollen and sweaty. His gloves dripped blood.

The shine from his trunks was so bright I could barely keep focused on him. He cracked his neck, never looking away from me. His lips stretched and blood oozed from the word *Morte* branded in his mouthpiece.

El Jefe's fist reared back.

"Wake up," he said to me.

Just when he was about to kill me with his punch, a hand squeezed my arm. I jerked away 'cause I couldn't see nothing but a shadow.

"Chula, wake up," said a voice from the dark of my room.

I reached for the light and turned it on.

"El Jefe?"

"Shhh, stay quiet," he said. "Only your father knows I'm here."

He put my wicker chair beside my bed and sat.

"But Richie said the papers—on TV . . ."

"Your tío hid me in a friend's basement," said El Jefe. "Your father asked me to come. He believes I am the reason you stopped taking your pills."

"I wanted to be strong," I said. "I didn't wanna be different no more."

His one eye fell to the floor and he rubbed his forehead like trying to mash out something he wished he hadn't thought.

"You don't know what it's like for everyone to hate you," I said. "To be weak and want to be strong. All of Mexico loves you, El Jefe. They throw lilies at you and the priests bless you with holy water. And all of the people chant your name—"

"It's a story, Chula. Look at me. Look at my face, my broken skin. Look at the scars all over me."

There were scars. Big gashes on his face. Slithering snakelike scars on his arms. But to look in his eye, I could imagine the other one beneath the patch. Imagine it as soft as the one I could see.

But I had been afraid. Afraid the minute he came to our door. Then it started coming to me. He was a man but he didn't really look like a man anymore. More like something cut up real bad and made into something else. Maybe people didn't love him. Maybe they—

"They're scared of you," I said, realizing it for the first time. "All of them. Not just us kids."

He nodded.

"But you are not scary, Chula. Different isn't bad. Your eyes are your eyes, not theirs. To be strong means to"—he searched for the word—"to accept what you are and love that."

There was such a big sadness in his eye. I could see his heart in there and it was hurting.

"El Jefe," I said. "Why did you kill the boy in Mexico?"

He exhaled real long. "My son, Fortino," said El Jefe, "was very strong and very large and very angry even as a little boy. His mama left us and we went from fight to fight, always winning enough for a while. A while is never long enough. When he was ten, he started running with a bad crowd, like your brother. They were older. Trouble had been their shadow from the day of their birth. Those boys filled my stomach with so much sickness . . ." He paused. "Fortino shot a man. A tourist, for a wallet of credit cards and seventy-nine dollars. His whole life my son had seen me fight and sometimes kill men to put food on our table. What was different between a gun and a fist? That was what he asked me."

I didn't know what to say. In no way did I know. El Jefe's face drew in tight and wrinkled along his eyes, squeezing into the shape of a rattlesnake's. All the hair on my arms stood up.

"He come in with his friends bragging how he killed that man," said El Jefe. "I told the boys to go but they started raising up all big. My son pointed his gun up at me to sit down. A ten-year-old boy barely old enough to dream and he waves a gun to his father? I hit him. I thought nothing of how hard and I didn't even know he wasn't moving. I turned on the boys with such rage and they ran. I'd never hit Fortino and just one time . . ." He breathed out real long again and the room chilled like a cold front had blown in.

"That was eleven years ago," said El Jefe. "But, for me, it is every second of every day."

"El Jefe?"

"Pablito," he said correcting me. "My name is Pablito, Chula."

I saw his suitcase sitting by the door.

"You're leaving," I said.

"I have to leave. I came here to help your Pape—your family. If the police come and find me, there would be trouble."

I didn't want him to go. Who would I talk to? Who would understand what it was like to be feared and not wanna be? Who would make me brave?

"Mi corazón promete," El Jefe said, "tu corazón."

"I don't understand."

"It means I cross this heart." And his voice shook as he made a light X on my chest. "Your heart."

My eyes got all sad and heavy and watery.

"I'll see you again," said El Jefe. "But now, ya no soy nada más. I am no more. Lo siento, Chula."

"We can hide—Pape will hide you."

He placed his thick scaly hand on my cheek and smiled like people do when they think they have to and their face don't wanna.

"You have such heart," said El Jefe. "It is magic."

"You didn't mean it," I said. "You didn't mean to kill Golden Gloves, right? You didn't mean to kill Fortino. It was an accident."

"We don't mean a lot of things in life," he said. "That doesn't make them right. Be strong. Sus ojos no son tus ojos."

The floorboards wailed and squealed as he made for my door. He picked up his suitcase and I started huffing and couldn't hold in the tears no longer. Then he was gone.

"Pablito?"

I don't remember falling asleep. Richie said to me the next morning that he came in the night to check on me and I was crying in my dreams and he woke me and I still cried and went to sleep only to cry again.

I didn't dream of Mexico. I dreamt of the earth. It was flat.

19

In the bathroom Monday morning, I poured one pink and a blue into my hand. I looked in the door mirror at me standing there holding the pills. Me, Chula Dolores Sanchez. Kinda pudgy but not fat. Kinda pretty even. I looked at myself real hard trying to find what everyone was so afraid of. What I was afraid of?

Richie banged on the door, shaking the mirror. "Andale, Chula. I'll meet you out on the porch."

I swallowed my pills and for the first time since

the accident prayed from my heart. Prayed to be brave like me . . . even with my head full of glass.

When I came out of the bathroom, Mama was putting towels up in the hall closet. We hadn't talked since Friday. We hadn't even looked at each other. Right then, it was just the two of us standing only a few feet apart but it was farther. A lot, lot farther.

Mama shut the closet and went into the kitchen.

Richie and me walked to school. Like always, him a few steps ahead. And like usual, he grabbed a stick and ran thumping it along the fences. And the dogs came barking crazy-like and Richie got up all close to one of the fences, showing his teeth back at one of them.

"Richie," I said.

"What?" he asked, still showing his wimpy teeth at the growling dog.

"Mama didn't say me nothing. Nothing at breakfast. Not even when I left."

"Ay, you know how she is."

"She looked at me like she does when I bring up Tía Josie."

He flung the stick to the dog he'd just been bugging.

"Come on." He started walking. "Pues, you just gotta let her be for a while. A couple of days, she'll be going on so much *you'll* start praying to the saints to make her stop."

"I'm serious, Richie."

"What do you want me to say?" he asked all annoyed.

"Forget it, don't say me nothing."

He reached up and yanked a handful of leaves off a tree. "I mean yeah, she's pissed at you 'cause you didn't take your pills. And she thinks she's doing everything right. By God, by the church, by Pape, by Abuela, and still we end up like this. Just getting by, you know."

"But don't that scare you? Knowing we ain't got nothing no more?"

He kinda laughed picking at the leaves. "Chula get for real. We never had nothing."

I stayed quiet. We had something. We had Pape walking and me without glass. We had more of Abuela's mind and we even had Richie looking forward to high school instead of repeating eighth grade. And even up until the week before, at least we had that three thousand dollars. That was something.

"Hey, relax, Chula," he said flinging leaf pieces on the ground. "If we have to beg, borrow, or lay away, we will. Besides, there's always a way to make money in the Circle."

"I just keep thinking there's gotta be a better way," I said.

"Than what?" he asked.

"Pues, no sé."

He grinned. "Check you out trying to speak Spanish. 'Pues, no sé.' Maybe there is hope for you, Chula."

We came around the corner to the bus stop bench where the dumb-head twins always met us. Only they weren't waiting.

"Where's Raul and Paul?" I asked Richie.

And before he could tell me we saw Freddy hanging at the end of the street.

"Be cool," Richie said to me. "When I say run, run to school."

"What's going on?" I asked, but it was too late 'cause Freddy was already heading right for us.

"Finally decided to show your face," Freddy said to Richie.

"Freddy man, listen—"

And that gel-headed rat grabbed Richie by the neck and dragged him into the alley.

"Run, Chula," Richie said.

I shook. I was so scared. I mean it. I started to back up. I started to run just like that night at the warehouse. Just like my brother had said.

Freddy punched Richie in the gut, slammed his fist into his jaw. Richie fell down.

I shook.

Everywhere.

All at once, I stormed right into that alley.

"Get outta here, pendeja," said Richie gasping for a breath.

Freddy made a point of me seeing the gun he had under his FUBU jacket.

"Get going, gorda," Freddy said. And he kicked Richie in the ribs. "Your brother knows why I'm pissed."

I shook. Everywhere.

"Leave him alone," I said.

Freddy half-laughed like he couldn't believe I said anything to him. That I was still standing there.

"Damn, Richie. Your fat little sister is tougher than you," said Freddy.

He knelt down and yanked Richie's slick black hair back so far I thought he might rip it right outta Richie's soft head.

"You *never* leave the guys in a fight," said Freddy. "Never."

"Man, they woulda threw me in juvie for sure if they caught me down there. My family, Freddy."

"We're your family," said Freddy. "I'm your brother, pendejo."

"No," I said. "He's MY brother, pendejo."

"Chula," said Richie.

Freddy stood up and could've been a ten-story brick building next to me.

"What you say to me, gorda?" asked Freddy stepping towards me.

"Leave my brother alone or I'll . . ." I paused.

What would I do? What could I do?

Freddy stepped closer. Then . . .

"I'll send the Cacooey," I said.

"Everyone knows he's gone." Freddy smirked.

"Maybe. But I know where to find him," I said.

He stopped walking.

"And he will kill you if you ever touch me or my brother again."

Freddy tried to see if I was bluffing him. I held my jaw so tight I thought I might crack every tooth in my mouth. But it was that or cry 'cause I was all kinds of scared.

Freddy backed up and pulled the gun from under his jacket.

"Richie," I said.

Freddy smashed the gun to Richie's head. Just when I thought he'd scatter Richie's thoughts all over the ground Freddy looked at me.

"What do I care," Freddy said.

Freddy tucked the gun back in his jeans. Richie crawled to his feet and staggered to me.

"Go, Richie," said Freddy. "But you're nothing in this neighborhood without me."

Richie and me backed out of the alley and didn't turn our backs to Freddy until we were around the corner.

"You know he doesn't believe you," said Richie.

"We're going to school, aren't we," I said.

I didn't take notes in Mr. Maskin's class 'cause for once it all made some kind of sense. He put the numbers on the board and asked questions and I actually knew the answers. Well, a lot of them. Jo looked at me like I was crazy but she looked at me like that a lot that day.

At lunch, I seen Ross the Floss go all the way to the back of the cafeteria and sit alone. If you were to ask me later why I stood up and walked over there, I couldn't say. The minute I got up to dump my untouched tray Jo couldn't stop staring. I felt it all the way past Carla's table and the Brain Reign. All the way to the back where the light just seemed darker somehow.

I went to the end of the table and sat across from Ross the Floss. He didn't even look up from his tray.

"Look, since Carla's gonna flatten me any second, you better start saying what you want," I said.

"It was stupid. Forget it," he said. "Nobody understands."

I looked over my shoulder and Carla was eagle-eying us like nuts.

"Okay, whatever," I said, getting up.

It wasn't worth getting my head beaten in if he wasn't even gonna ask me nothing.

"She's scared of you."

"What?"

"My sister. She's scared of you."

"She don't act scared."

Carla came up to the table. I looked over my shoulder and Jo and Mary Alice started to get up.

"Go away, Carla," said Ross.

She looked at me and said, "I told you to stay away—"

"Go away!" he shouted, flying outta his chair. *"Leave!"*

I don't know if she was more shocked than me. I never imagined anything that loud coming outta Ross the Floss. Carla looked back at Royal Rich. They were kinda laughing at how her little brother made her look all stupid.

"Fine," she said. "I'm done helping you."

"Good," he said.

I wasn't moving for nothing. Even when she was all the way back to her chair I was still standing there. Jo held up her hands like "What's up?" as her and Mary Alice got up to go. I looked down at Ross sitting back down staring at his tray. I sat back down and waited for him to say something.

"When you were in that car accident, it was bad, right?"

I shrugged. "Yeah."

"And you have seizures because of it."

I nodded.

His face was so quiet. So serious.

"My dad died last year. And my mom, she's sick a lot lately," he said. "And she started having these seizures, only she won't really talk about it. I thought . . . you could tell me what it's like. Or what to do? Or say?"

I sat there with my eyes trying to find somewhere to drop. I didn't know what to be telling him about his mom.

"Forget it," he said.

"Just hold on, okay?" I inhaled real deep and felt the air shake outta me. "Like I don't even know what to tell you. I mean, we don't talk about it in my house."

"But taking the medicine, it stops the seizures from happening?" he asked. "I mean, that's what it said on the Internet."

"I don't know. I never looked it up like that. I mean, I'm not supposed to Flash, have seizures, when I take the medication. But the doctor said the pills were more like an insurance policy. That didn't make no sense to me till my father said the

201

pills are protection. He says it's not a promise but a chance. A real good one. I don't know, maybe he's right."

He was so focused on what I was saying I didn't know what to do. I thought I'd just blush or stick out my tongue or go running out as fast as possible. But I just, I don't know, got real steady inside.

"She had a real big seizure," said Ross. "Last week. Carla was at the mall and I didn't know what to do. I saw the teachers put you on your side when you got sick the first week of school, so I did that. But I was so scared."

His brow drew in real tight. He looked at me so hard. Harder than anyone ever looked at me.

"I think whatever's wrong it's bad, you know," said Ross. "I don't want my mom to die too."

Ay, did it get all quiet between us. There was the banging of forks on the plastic trays and muddied gossip and laughing all around us. But it was just nothing, noise in the background of a sound of something that wasn't glass. It was his heart, breaking.

"I could ask my mom to light a candle," I said. "She's really big on that."

Then something changed. He kinda smiled. I mean, not real big but soft.

I sat there thinking, I really would ask Mama to light a candle. Maybe even two 'cause it sounded like he needed it. Mama didn't need to know he was a gringo. "God hears all prayers," said Abuela once. "God sees all colors. That's why he made them so beautiful."

"I'll see you," said Ross, picking up his tray. "Thanks, Chula."

He tipped his tray over the garbage and pushed through the double doors. I would've thought I imagined the whole thing if Carla hadn't spun around in her seat to look at me. It seemed like a forever that we looked at each other before she turned back around. Maybe not everything was round or square. I mean, there is geometry and they got all kinds of shapes.

20

i did algebra and got halfway through this book we gotta finish by the end of the semester in Saturday class. Richie met me at the school and went with me to Mary Alice's party. The minute we walked in you could see it cost *a lot* of money. There were matching streamers and tablecloths. Big helium balloons and a two-story cake in the shape of, well, I don't know really what it was because I was late and they'd already cut into it. The food was fancy and on crackers and special chips and like everyone and their dog came just like

Mary Alice had said all along. But I don't know. It just seemed boring somehow.

After Mary Alice's birthday, the days went by fast. Halloween fell into Thanksgiving. Then pues, all the jingles and lights of Christmas running along the houses came. Mama got a better job in Squaretown working at a hotel restaurant and Pape started working for this business that wanted him to call people a lot. But nothing, nothing of El Jefe.

When school started back again in January, Jo, Mary Alice, and me, we hung out less and less until one day I was sitting in Mr. Maskin's class and realized when he called her name Jo hadn't been there in a week. She started running with the Dark Skins and after that I don't know. She just wasn't around.

Richie got caught just weeks before the end of junior high pulling off a robbery with the Dark Skins. He can't get out of juvie until he's seven-teen. I miss him a lot. I read to him over the phone when he calls. Read to him about Mexico. He even smiles sometimes. I can feel it.

At the seventh- and eighth-grade awards as-sembly, I got this certificate that said:

I looked out into the crowd and saw Mama, Pape, Tío Tony, and even Abuela. Her head back looking into the rafters of the gym, staring at the lights . . . singing softly to the moon probably. Even Tía Josie was there way in the back, away from the rest of the family but close enough that maybe someday we could all be closer. I couldn't help but to smile when I looked deep into the happy faces and clapping hands. When I looked into a part of the gym that was really dark, a small corner just big enough to notice, I seen something move there. Something big with skin like caramel that sat in the sun too long and got all dried and hard in places. I saw the white of two eyes, not one, and a large, kind grin. It was only for a moment that I saw that in the darkness but it might as well been an hour 'cause I carry that feeling with me. So that I say to myself, "Mi corazón promete tu corazón." And sometimes before bed when I close my eyes, the noise of the Circle fades and what I hear begins as a whisper, a low roar of a crowd chanting, "Jefe! Jefe!"

glossary of
spanish words

abuela (ah•BWAY•lah): grandmother

abuelo (ah•BWAY•loh): grandfather

ay dios mio (eye DEE•ohs MEE•oh): oh my God

andale (AHN•da•lay): hurry up

bueno (BWAY•noh): good

buenos noches (BWAY•nos NOH•chays): Good night

Cacooey (ka•COO•ee): mythical Mexican boogeyman

callate (KAI•yah•tay): be quiet

carne guisada (KAHR•nay gwee•SAH•dah): Mexican dish of meat and gravy often served inside a flour tortilla.

chorizo (chor•EE•zoh): Mexican sausage

¿Cómo estás? (KOH•moh eh•STAHS): How are you?

¿Comprende? (kom•PREN•day): understand?

coyote (kai•YOH•tee): (English) person who brings people to the United States from Mexico illegally

¿Dónde está? (DON•day eh•STAH): Where is . . . ?

en mi cama (en mee KAH•mah): in my bed

frijoles (free•HOL•es): beans

gorda (GOR•dah): fat (a girl)

gracias (GRAH•see•ahs): thank you

gringa (GREEN•gah): white female

gringo (GREEN•goh): white male

huevos (OOWAY•vos): eggs

el jefe (el HEH•fay): the boss

las raspadas (las rahs•PAH•dahs): snow cones

loco (LOH•koh): crazy

lo siento (loh see•EHN•toh): I'm sorry

maracas (mahr•AH•kahs): Mexican musical instrument

mi familia (mee fah•MEE•lee•ah): my family

mi'ja (MEE•hah): my child (a girl)

mi'jo (MEE•hoh): my child (a boy)

morte (MORT•ay): death

no sé (no say): I don't know

ocico (oh•SEE•koh): rude slang term for "shut your mouth"

ojo (oh•hoh): eye

pan dulce (pahn DUHL•say): sweet bread

papas (PAH•pahs): potatoes

pendejo/a (pen•DAY•hoh/hah): (very rude) stupid

pobrecita (POH•bray•SEE•tah): poor baby (a girl)

por favor (por fah•VOR): please

¿Por qué? (por kay): Why?

pues (pways): but; well

¿Qué pasó? (kay pah•SOH): What's up?

sangria (san•GREE•ah): red wine and brandy with pieces of fruit

silencio (sih•LEN•see•oh): silence

sopapillas (soh•pah PEE•yahs): Mexican dessert of fried bread, often covered with honey and cinnamon

tamale (tah•MAH•lay): cornmeal dough filled with meat, wrapped in a corn husk

taquito (tah•KEE•toh): corn or flour tortilla filled and deep-fried

te ayudaré (tay ai•YOO•dahr•AY): I'll help you

tejano (tay•HAH•noh): style of music that combines Texan and Mexican melodies

telenovela (TEH•leh•no•VEH•lah): Mexican soap opera

tía (TEE•ah): aunt

tío (TEE•oh): uncle

y, olé (ee oh•LAY): (slang) oh my God

Extraspecial thanks to:
Pat Schmatz, an amazing children's writer whose
dedication to *Prizefighter en Mi Casa*'s potential
was unwavering.

Gracias:
Kurt and Anouck Struyf
Galen T. McGriff
Karen Dodson
Sandra Silva
Paul "Popcorn" Charlton
Lea Hilzinger
Betty Thomas
Dr. Christopher Zuzzio
Boston's City Girl Café
Margaret Coble
John "The Bear" Butler
Dr. Elizabeth Mermann-Joziwick
Vanessa Jackson
Patrick Zapata
Amanda J. Cunningham
My absolutely amazing editor, Krista Marino

And the countless filmmakers, playwrights, and
authors who continue to inspire me . . .

Born and raised in south Texas, e. E. Charlton-Trujillo started writing as soon as she could type. When she was a teenager, a sports injury forced her back to the typewriter, then soon to the stage, earning her a scholarship to Texas A&M, after which she went on to Ohio University for an MFA in film. Before writing *Prizefighter en Mi Casa,* Charlton-Trujillo was a playwright, a screenwriter, and an award-winning writer and director of short films. She now resides in Madison, Wisconsin, where, if she's not reading three books at once, she's dreaming of palm trees and the Gulf of Mexico.